"Are You Taking The Deal Or Not?"

Ethan sat back in his chair and regarded her with cold blue eyes.

Mary had never seen a man with more arrogance—or more presence—than this one. "I told you I'd agree to artificial insemination."

"I know what you told me." His sapphire gaze missed nothing, especially her intense desire to stop him. "But to make sure your end of the bargain is upheld, we'll do this the old-fashioned way."

"Not a chance in hell."

He looked amused. "You might even like it...."

P9-APJ-078

Dear Reader,

The truth is I love the alpha male. I love reading about him, writing about him and being married to him. I believe this obsession started in high school, where in my senior year I realized that the guys who grew up to be driven, highly intelligent, take-charge, sexy alpha males were not the popular high school boys I'd hoped would notice me. No, those guys were peaking too soon. Our men, our Mr. Darcy's, were the quiet ones, intense and driven in their pursuits.

In the first book of my series, NO RING REQUIRED, we meet the alpha of all alphas: Ethan Curtis. "Driven in his pursuits" takes on a whole new meaning for this self-made millionaire, who has only one unfulfilled goal left to pursue—to have a blue-blooded child. Ethan will do anything to get what he wants, and if he has to blackmail a beautiful blonde in the process, so be it....

Enjoy!

Laura

LAURA WRIGHT

MILLIONAIRE'S CALCULATED BABY BID

Published by Silhouette Books
America's Publisher of Contemporary Romance

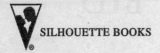

SILHOUETTE BOOKS

ISBN-13: 978-0-373-76828-8
ISBN-10:   0-373-76828-1

MILLIONAIRE'S CALCULATED BABY BID

Recent Books by Laura Wright

Silhouette Desire

Redwolf's Woman #1582
A Bed of Sand #1607
The Sultan's Bed #1661
Her Royal Bed #1674
Savor the Seduction #1687
*Millionaire's Calculated Baby Bid #1828

*No Ring Required

LAURA WRIGHT

has spent most of her life immersed in the world of acting, singing and competitive ballroom dancing. But when she started writing romance, she knew she'd found her true calling! Although born and raised in Minneapolis, Laura has also lived in New York, Ohio and Wisconsin. Currently, she has set down her bags in Los Angeles, California, and although the town can be a little crazy at times, Laura is grateful to have her theatrical production manager husband, two young children and three dogs to keep her sane.

During her downtime from writing, Laura loves to paint, play peek-a-boo with her little boy, go to movies with her husband and read with her daughter. She loves hearing from her readers and can be reached at P.O. Box 57523 Sherman Oaks, CA. 91413.

For Lucca Elliott, my sweet baby boy…

Prologue

One hour ago Mary had expected to lie back on the king-size bed in the most exclusive bed-and-breakfast in Long Lake, Minnesota, and let Ethan Curtis make love to her, with no emotion, zero response from her body. At that very same time, she'd wondered if he'd be rough, cold, like the unfeeling bastard she'd met in her family's former offices a week ago—the offices he now controlled and ran like a well-oiled, profit-gouging, soul-sucking machine.

His mouth moved over hers, slowly, seductively coaxing her back to the present. Every time his skin brushed against hers, every time his teeth raked lightly over her neck or back or shoulder, she mewled so loudly with desire she was sure the entire inn heard her and knew exactly what she was doing.

Ethan Curtis might've been a bastard, but he was anything but cold.

Moonlight spilled into the room, making it impossible not to see Ethan's face as he pushed into her again, his cut cheekbones, hard mouth, and tanned neck taut with exertion and damp with sweat. His cobalt gaze slipped from her eyes to her mouth, and he lowered his head. Mary's heart hammered in her chest as she tried to force back the rush of desire in her blood when his full mouth found hers and nuzzled her lips open.

The reality of why they were here in bed together, so that her father was now free from any threat of prison, scratched at the door of her mind. She wished she could crawl out from underneath Ethan and leave the room, but her body continued to betray her. Maybe it was because she hadn't been with a man in two years. Maybe she just craved the weight and the closeness and the surge of adrenaline, but she wanted this man so badly she ached with it.

Ethan drifted lazily from her mouth to her cheek, then to her ear. She felt the tip of his tongue against her lobe and shivered, her back arching, her hips arching, her body taking him deeper. Her ears were surprisingly sensitive, and she hated that he knew it, that he was having this power over her—yet loved it at the same time. His tongue flicked back and forth as though he were tending to more than just the lobe of her ear, and she trembled again with sudden spasms she couldn't control. Outside their door, she heard voices, heavy footfall in the hallway, then a door closing. Had they heard her as she moaned with desire, her body begging him for more?

The urge to touch Ethan, grab his lower back and buttocks, sink her fingers and nails into his muscular flesh was almost overwhelming and she fisted the sheets at her sides. It was the one thing she'd promised herself—not to touch him. But the pledge was hurting her far more than it was hurting him, she imagined. His tanned, thickly muscled chest and shoulders had erotic voices of their own and were calling to her as he rose for a moment, then settled back against her breasts.

How could you sleep with a man like this? she heard herself say, though the only sound her throat produced was a deep moan of satisfaction as he lowered his head to her breast and suckled deeply on one hard, pink nipple. *How could you desire a man like this?*

He's a demon.

Shuddering with the electric heat, she wrapped her legs around him and arched her back, pumping her hips furiously. She was close, so close. It had been two incredibly quiet years since she'd been with a man she'd dated for only a few months, two long years since she'd faked release before breaking it off and wandering back into hermit territory and remaining there as the eternal businesswoman. She'd felt the real charge of climax only in her dreams—those dreams of faceless strangers pleasuring her body until she woke up sweaty and frustrated. But there was no faking anything tonight.

Again her thoughts were seized and cast aside by Ethan's touch. He slipped his hand between them, his fingers inching downward until he combed through the pale curls between her spread thighs. As he stroked her, flicked the tender, aching bud, Mary gulped for air. She didn't want to give in to him. He didn't deserve her desire, her complete and utter surrender. But her head fell back anyway as the heat of his hand and the skill of his fingers took her over the edge. She knew how loudly she cried out as he played her, as he sank deeper, but she didn't care. Wounded, desperate and totally unaware of time, she clawed at the white sheets, pretending they were his skin.

Ethan watched her, his gaze feral yet brushed with uncharacteristic concern. Then with a growl of hunger, he pushed deeply inside her, his rhythm steady, his breathing anything but. The force of his release made him shake, made his body hard as iron, and when he dropped gently on top of her, he buried his head in the damp curve of her neck.

It was only moments before Mary's skin started to cool and her rational mind returned, along with her anger. No matter how much her body craved this man, in the light of day this had been little more than a transaction.

A wave of nausea moved through her as she recalled the day Ethan Curtis had made her an offer she hadn't been able to refuse.

"You're one arrogant son of a bitch, you know that, Curtis?" she had said to him.

Ethan had sat back in his leather chair and regarded her with cold eyes. "I think we've established that. Are you going to take the deal or not?"

With his short black hair, sharp blue eyes and hooked nose, Ethan resembled a hawk more than a man. Mary had never seen a man with more arrogance or more presence.

She had stood in his massive office of glass and metal, with its hard, uncompromising edges, and tried to be as much of a hard-ass as him. "I told you I would agree to artificial insemination."

"If I felt that you would actually honor—"

"Honor?" she said, appalled. "We've leaped way beyond that now."

"True." His sapphire gaze had missed nothing, especially the intense desire she had to thwart him in any way possible. "But to make certain your end of the bargain is upheld, we'll do this the old-fashioned way."

"Not a chance in hell."

He'd looked amused. "You may even like it."

She'd given him a derisive glance. "Maybe. But we'll never know. I'm not going to bed with you, Mr. Curtis."

The look of amusement had disappeared and he'd replied gravely, "You want your father cleared of all charges. I want a child. It's very simple."

Simple. The word now crashed around in Mary's brain as the man who'd uttered it one week ago rolled off her in one gentle movement. Nothing was simple about this situation. She ventured a quick glance at him as he sat up, his back to her, ropes of thick muscle flexing as he moved. Was it possible to despise someone yet be intrigued by them at the same time?

His voice cut through her silent query. "Do you want me to go?"

Despite her efforts to remain indifferent, she felt anger bubble up within her. At herself and at him. "Yes."

His jaw tight, he let out a slow breath. "I *will* see you again tomorrow."

Without answering, she got up from the bed and headed straight for the bathroom. She wasn't about to turn over and lie there, sheet pulled up to her chin like a naive girl who'd just been taken advantage of. She'd known exactly what she was doing and why, and had admittedly enjoyed herself.

She turned on the shower to drown out any sound of him getting dressed and walking out, then threw back the shower curtain and stared at the water as it dropped like rain onto the virginal white surface of the porcelain tub. She placed one foot over the tub, but quickly stepped back on the mat. Why the hell wasn't she getting in there, getting clean, getting rid of any sign of him? What kind of woman didn't want to wash off the scent of a man she had sworn to hate—a man who wanted her only to procure a blue-blooded child? Not any kind of woman she would respect.

Mary let go of the curtain and went to stand in front of the full-length mirror on the bathroom door. With nervous fingers, she ran a hand down her torso, over her belly. Had they made a child tonight? A shiver of excitement went through her, accompanied by an intense feeling of dread. A baby. She sighed. There was nothing in the world she wanted more than to build a family of her own, but not this way.

Feeling ashamed, she looked away. Her priorities were what they had always been, ever since she was a child: to fix the lives of others before her own. And right now having all charges dropped against her father was the most important thing. She wasn't getting a family out of this deal, she was keeping her father out of prison.

Her hands splayed on her belly once more and she shook her head. Impossible. The whole damn deal. She was a fool for thinking it would work, just as Ethan Curtis was a fool for thinking that if she did get pregnant, the baby would ever be raised by anyone but its mother.

One

Four Weeks Later.

"**W**hose idea was it to install a kitchen in the office?" Tess York inquired, the words slightly muffled by a massive bite of eggs Benedict.

Olivia Winston flipped a yellow dish towel over her shoulder and walked her petite, though incredibly curvaceous, frame over to the table with the grace of a movie star. "Ah, that would be me."

"Well, you're a genius, kid."

Beneath a rim of shaggy brown bangs, Olivia's gold eyes sparkled. "This I know."

Tess laughed at her partner's mock display of arrogance, her long mass of red curls hopping about her back like marionettes. "All I want to know is where my mimosa is."

"No drinking before ten o'clock." Mary Kelley sat across from Tess, her wavy blond hair falling about her face as she absentmindedly drew slash marks through the hollandaise with her fork. "Unless disaster strikes."

"I'd say a two-week dry spell qualifies," Tess said slyly, making Olivia laugh.

"It's August." Mary looked from one of her partners to the other. "We're always a little slow at the end of the summer."

"Slow, sure," Olivia retorted, holding a piece of perfectly cooked bacon up like a white flag. "But we're bordering on drought."

Barring these two weeks in August, No Ring Required was normally buzzing with activity. The premier wife-for-hire company in the Midwest had zero competition and one hell of a brilliant staff. With Mary's creativity and business sense, Olivia's culinary skill and Tess's wise budgeting and decorating style, NRR was a highly successful company. The problem, Mary had to admit, was that all three of them were such intense workaholics who cared nothing for a private life that they had no idea what to do with themselves on their downtime. And each time the end of summer came aknocking, the women panicked in their own ways.

"Well," Mary continued, putting down her fork and dropping her napkin over an untouched plate of food. "Clearly this is no time to be picky about clients."

"Yeah, Olivia," Tess murmured with a grin.

Olivia raised her brows questioningly. "And what is that supposed to mean?"

"I think she's referring to your problem with trust-fund clients," Mary offered, laughing when Tess cleared her throat loudly.

Olivia scowled, then reached down and grabbed Mary's plate. "I don't like them, and nothing's going to change that. Trust-funders are boorish, brainless, self-obsessed jerks, who think they not only own the world, but everyone else along with it."

Tess flashed Mary a grin. "Tell us how you really feel."

"Yes," Mary agreed. "I'm not entirely clear on your opinion regarding the rich."

As her partners chuckled, Olivia sighed. "It's not the rich, it's— Oh, forget it." Clearly looking for a way to end the current conversation, Olivia glared at Mary's untouched plate. "Mary, you're not on a diet, are you?"

"What?" Mary said, sobering.

Olivia tossed her an assessing glance before she turned and sashayed back to her beloved Viking range. "You know that I feel as though diets are a total affront to all those in the culinary world."

"I do know that."

"Besides, there's not a grapefruit or bowl of cabbage soup in my fridge, I'm afraid."

As a shot of nerves zipped through her, Mary shook her head. "No diet, Olivia. I guess I'm just not very hungry."

Tess paused long enough to swallow. "As much as I hate to side with Olivia, that's been going on for a while now."

"Yep," Olivia agreed.

"And, well," Tess began awkwardly, "we're here if…well, you know."

Mary nodded and forced a smile. "I know."

Among the three of them, talking about business was an easy, playful and spirited adventure, but when the conversation turned to anything emotional or personal, the women of NRR seemed to transform into the Stooges—a bumbling, uneasy mess. From the inception of No Ring Required there had been a sort of unspoken rule between the partners to keep personal matters to themselves. Odd, and perhaps against every female cliché, for three women to abstain from discussion about history and feelings, but there it was.

"So, what's on the agenda today, ladies?" Tess asked, pushing away from the table and a very clean plate.

"I have a meeting with a potential client," Mary informed them, her gaze drifting over to the clock on the wall. Okay, five minutes were up. The test was done. The zip of nerves from a moment ago turned into a pulse-pounding elephant-sitting-on-her-chest type of situation.

"Maybe not such a dry spell after all," Olivia remarked gaily, her good mood returning. "I also have a client coming in at two whose fiancée ditched him a week before the wedding and he wants help with what he referred to as a "screw her" dinner party."

Tess laughed. "Should be fun."

Mary hardly heard them as the muscles in her legs tensed painfully, as though she was on the verge of a charley horse. The pregnancy test was hidden behind fifty or so rolls of the insanely soft Charmin Ultra that

Olivia insisted on buying. Would there be one line or two? One line or two?

"Big name or big business for you?" Tess asked, staring at Mary expectantly.

"Ah…both actually."

"Sounds great." Olivia set her own full plate down beside Tess, then promptly rearranged her silverware, napkin and water glass to their proper places, now ready to partake in her own breakfast.

Her heart slamming against her ribs, Mary stood and grabbed her purse. "I just have to hit the little girl's room and then I'll be on my way."

"Good luck," Olivia called.

Tess nodded. "Yeah, good luck, kid."

If they only knew the double meaning in her good wishes, Mary thought, each step toward the bathroom feeling as though she was walking in quicksand. She had no idea what she wanted to see when she tossed aside all that toilet paper and pulled out the test. If it was positive, she'd have to make plans to get away from Minneapolis eventually, away from Ethan—that man would never let her walk away with his child. If it was negative, her father's life was over. She felt a sickly sour feeling in her stomach. She had lives to protect, and she wasn't altogether sure how capable she was.

She locked the door behind her, sat on the floor and opened the cabinets under the sink. The mountain of white rolls pushed aside easily as she reached inside and felt for the thin stick. Her pulse pounded in her ears. God, what did she want here?

Her fingers closed around the test and she yanked it back. With one heavy exhale she stared at the results.

It was three twenty-seven and Ethan Curtis was growing more impatient by the second.

He wasn't used to being kept waiting. People arrived early for meetings with him, fifteen to thirty minutes on average. They would sit in his massive lobby until he was ready to see them. For six years it had been this way. He knew his employees thought he was an arrogant ass. He liked it that way.

He punched the intercom button. "Marylyn, when Miss Kelley arrives, have her join me on the roof."

There was a slight pause on the other end of the line. Marylyn had never heard such a request, but she recovered quickly. "Yes, sir. Of course."

Ethan glanced at the clock. Three thirty-one. Where the hell was she? He stalked over to the elevator and stabbed the button. Mary Kelley was a strong-willed, business-first, no-nonsense type of person—not unlike himself. But if she worked for him, she'd be fired by now.

He was not generally a nervous man. He didn't pace, worry or stress before a deal was done. If a client didn't perform or comply the way he wanted them to, he finessed the situation, made it work to his advantage. However, as he rode his private elevator the short distance to the roof, his gut continued to contract painfully, just like it had the day his father had informed him that his mother had taken up with a new man and wasn't coming back.

Ethan walked out of the elevator and onto the rooftop, for which he had hired a world-renowned landscape architect and two botanists to transform into his escape three years ago. The courtyard opened to a Moroccan-tiled fountain and several ancient sculptures, while to the left was a sun terrace, complete with bar and circular planters filled with flax, pyracantha and perennials to keep the urban scene colorful year-round. Red bougainvillea covered several of the arched trellises, and cherry trees flanked the central walkway. It was a strange mixture of ease and exotic, and it suited Ethan perfectly.

He sensed her, smelled her, before he saw her. Fresh, soapy—yes, he remembered. The lower half of him contracted as his mind played the ever-present film of those nights in July over again. Ethan saw himself lying on top of her, buried deep inside of her, his mouth on hers as he breathed in her scent and she moaned and writhed like a wildcat.

He glanced over his shoulder to see her walking toward him. She was average height, average build, but Mary Kelley possessed two things that would make any man stop dead in his tracks and stare. Long, toned, sexy-as-hell legs that he could practically feel wrapped around his waist at this moment, and pale blue eyes that turned up at the corners, like a cat's. "You're late."

She didn't respond. "What's all this, Mr. Curtis?" she said, looking around the garden seemingly unimpressed. "Your bat cave?"

As well as the legs and the eyes, she also had a sharp tongue.

"A sanctuary."

Her brows drew together as she sat in the chair opposite him, the skirt of her pale blue Chanel suit sliding upward to just a few inches above her knees. The late-afternoon sun hit her full force, her blond hair appearing almost white. "And what do you need sanctuary from? All the people you've screwed over this week?"

Yes, a very sharp tongue, though he remembered that it could also be soft and wet. "You think I thrive on making life difficult for others?"

"I think it may be your life's blood."

There was no disputing the fact that she disliked him. No, he could see that clearly. What he couldn't make out from her attitude was if she was carrying his child or not, and that was the one thing he desperately wanted to know.

He walked over to the bar. "Drink?"

She nodded. "Thank you."

"Anything in particular? Martini, soda?" That would give him his answer.

"Something cold would be nice. It's pretty warm."

"You're going to make me work for this, aren't you?"

"Would you really appreciate it any other way?" she said brusquely.

"Martini?"

"Lemonade would be great if you have it. I'm driving."

"Mary—"

"Do you think you deserve an easy answer, Mr. Curtis?" she interrupted coldly. "Think back to how we got here."

He had done nothing but, for the past four weeks, though not in the same way as she, clearly. "We made an agreement."

She laughed bitterly. "Is that what you'd call it? You blackmailed me and I gave in. Maybe gave up is a better way to put it."

Ethan abandoned the drinks and went to stand before her. Her cat eyes were blazing hatred, and her claws were out, but he didn't give a damn if she was angry. He wanted one thing and one thing only, and he would go to any lengths necessary to get it.

"Are you pregnant?" he asked bluntly.

It took her a moment to answer. Several emotions crossed her face, and her breathing seemed shallow and slightly labored before she finally nodded. "Yes."

Ethan turned away, his heart pounding like a jack-hammer. He'd wanted this but had never believed it possible. He had no idea how to react.

"You'll drop all charges against my father," Mary said, her tone nonemotional.

He stood there, his back to her. "Of course."

"And you won't interfere in my life until the baby is born."

He opened his mouth to agree, then paused. He turned to face her again. "I don't know if can do that."

"That was our agreement," Mary countered, coming to her feet, her gaze fierce. "Do you not even have one ounce of honor in your blood, Mr. Curtis? Where the hell did you grow up, under a rock?"

She didn't know where he came from, couldn't know,

but her words struck him hard and he frowned. "I will keep my word."

Seemingly satisfied, Mary grabbed her purse and started for the elevator. "Good."

"But there's one condition," Ethan called after her.

She whirled around, held his gaze without blinking. "There were no conditions."

"This has nothing to do with my child, Mary. This is business."

"I was under the impression that the child was business," she said dryly.

Despite the dig, Ethan pressed on. "I want to hire you."

She looked confused for a moment, then broke out laughing bitterly. "Never."

"You'd turn away business so you don't have to be around me? I thought you were way tougher than that."

"I have enough business. I don't need yours."

The foolishness of that statement made him smile. "Being the heads of two successful companies, we both know that's not true."

"Look," she began impatiently, "my deal with you is done. Unless you plan to go back on your word and not drop the charges—"

"No," he cut in firmly. "But perhaps you also want that sculpture your father risked so much to retrieve?"

"I couldn't give a damn."

"No, but your father does." He gestured to the courtyard and the small sculpture of a woman and child that Hugh Kelley had almost gone to jail for. It had been a gift from the Harringtons, part of their courtship when Ethan took over the company. They'd hated him for buying controlling shares in Harrington Corp., but the company was floundering under their care, and because they still wanted to be involved, they'd forced themselves to act nicely. If Ethan had known the rare sculpture belonged to a family member, he probably would've rejected the piece. For as much as he wanted to be accepted and welcomed into the old money of Minneapolis, he hated family drama. He hadn't been too keen on having Hugh Kelley arrested for wanting the sculpture back, either, but he also wouldn't allow breaking and entering at his company for any reason.

"Why are you doing this?" Mary asked, her cat eyes inspecting him as though he were a pesky rodent. "Why would you care if my father has that sculpture back? You have what you want."

A pink blush stained her cheeks. She was so beautiful, and her temper and passion only made her more so. She was kidding herself and him if she thought they were done with each other. Two things had come out of their nights together: a baby and the desire to have her in his bed again. Both would take time, but he'd get what he wanted.

"I want to be there," he said simply. "I want to be around you and see what's happening to you. I want to see this child grow. That's all." When she said nothing, he moved on. "I have several parties to give and to attend over the next month. And one trip—"

"Trip?" she interrupted.

"To Mackinac Island."

"Not a chance."

"You don't travel with clients?"

"You're not a client."

"Listen, if it were simply a business meeting, I'd go alone, but I have to stay a few days and I'm planning on throwing a party as well."

"And you could find someone to help you with that anywhere," she said. "Some woman you know? And I'm sure you know several."

His mouth twitched with amusement. "I do."

"A girlfriend."

"No."

"How about a call girl then?" she suggested, flashing him a sarcastic grin.

"I want the best. A professional—and NRR has a sterling reputation. And, quite honestly, it wouldn't hurt having a Harrington by my side to—"

"Right," she said quickly, then shook her head. "I don't think so."

She was so damn stubborn. "Do you know the circles I run in?"

"I could guess."

"The kind that are really good for your business."

She shrugged, shook her head again.

He stepped closer, studied her, then grinned. "You're afraid of what might happen if you're around me."

"Try concerned." She walked away, over to the bar where she poured herself a glass of iced tea. "Listen, Mr. Curtis, I won't deny my attraction to you, just like I won't deny my abhorrence of you, either."

"I appreciate your honesty. But that's still—"

"A no."

"Well your refusal doesn't take away from the fact that I need help. I could ask one of your partners—"

She fairly choked on her tea. "No."

Ethan hesitated. It was the first time he'd seen her ruffled during their conversation. Sex didn't shake her up emotionally, and neither did money, business or the subject of her father, but just mentioning her partners at NRR had her sweating.

"You have two partners, isn't that right?" he asked casually.

"They know nothing about you…or this," she said in a caustic tone. "And I want it to stay that way."

"I see."

She put down her glass and stood at the side of the bar. "You want your eyes on me all the time…"

"For starters."

She nodded slowly, as though she were thinking. "All right, Mr. Curtis. You get what you want once again. I'll take the job." She turned away then, and walked to the elevator. "But understand something," she added as the door slid open. "What happened at the lake will never happen again."

"Whatever you say, Mary," Ethan said with a slow grin as the elevator door closed.

It was seven o'clock on the nose when Mary walked into the little Craftsman house at 4445 Gabby Street. She'd grown up there, happy as any girl could be with two parents who adored her and told her so every day. With two such gentle souls guiding her, she should have been a softer, sweeter personality, but clearly there was too much Harrington in her. Instead of hugs, she loved to argue and battle and win. Today at Ethan Curtis's office she'd done all three fairly well. She'd won her dad's freedom, though she'd paid a high price for it.

Mary walked through the house, then out the screen door. She knew where her father was. During sunset, Hugh Kelley always sat in the backyard, his butt in dirt and under a shifting sky, he patted the newly sprung string bean plants as though they were his children. He was sixty-five, but lately he looked closer to seventy-five, far from the strapping man he used to be. Today was no different. He looked old and weathered, his gray hair too long in the back. For the millionth time Mary wondered if he would ever recover from her mother's long illness and death and the arrest that followed. She hoped her news would at the very least remove a few layers of despair.

He glanced up from his beans and grinned. "Never been late in your life, have you, lass?"

Her father's Irish brogue wrapped around her like a soft sweater. "If there was one thing you taught me, Pop, it was punctuality."

"What a load of crap."

Mary laughed and plunked down beside him in the dirt.

"Watch yourself there." Hugh gestured to the ground. "That suit will be black as coal dust by the time you leave."

"I'm all right, Pop."

He snapped a bean from its vine and handed it to her.

"And you know I haven't been on time a day in my life. Neither had your mother. Not you, though. Born right on your due date, you were. Neither your mother nor I ever understood where your timeliness came from. Well, no place we'd admit to, certainly."

Hugh wasn't being cryptic, just matter-of-fact. The rift between Mary's father and her grandparents was old news—though old news he loved to drum up again and again. Not that she blamed him. The Harringtons had never approved of him, and had made him feel like an Irish peasant from day one. Mary just wished things could've been different all around. Bitterness and resentment were such a waste of time.

She took a bite of her bean as the late-summer breeze played with her hair. "So, I have some news."

"What's that, lass?"

"Ethan Curtis has dropped the charges."

Hugh didn't look surprised. "So my lawyer informs me."

"You already knew?"

"Yep. Teddy called me half an hour ago."

Mary studied his expression. Unchanged, tired, defeated. She shook her head. "Why aren't you happy, relieved, something?"

"I am something." His pale blue eyes, so like her own, brightened with passion. "I'm pissed off."

"What? Why?"

"I know you, lass. I know you better than anyone. What did you do to make this happen?"

Her heart jumped into her throat, but she remained

cool as steel on the outside. "I don't know what you're talking about."

"Mare."

"Pop, I talked to the man."

Hugh snorted. "Ethan Curtis is no man. He's a devil, a demon with no soul."

Mary was all set to agree when a memory of the cozy room on Lake Richard flashed into her mind. Ethan was a demon, yes, but there was another side to him—a deeply buried side that held a surprising amount of warmth and tenderness. She'd seen it when he'd talked about his child.

She closed her eyes. *His child.*

"Well he's decided to let it go," Mary forced out. "He agreed that the sculpture wasn't really worth his time and is even willing to give it back to you. After all, it was just a gift from Grandmother, with zero sentimental value to him and—"

"A gift that old woman had no right to give," Hugh pointed out gruffly.

Mary gave a patient sigh. "I know, Pop."

The basket beside him strained with vegetables. No doubt he'd been out here picking for a few hours. Lord only knew what he was going to do with it all. "Promise me you're not in any trouble."

Mary's chin lifted. She'd lied, yes, but she'd done what she had to do. She was no more pregnant than a box of rocks, but her father was free, and protecting him was all she cared about right now.

"I have nothing to fear from Ethan Curtis," she said

tightly. As long as he didn't find out the truth, she amended silently, as she picked up the basket of vegetables and walked inside the house.

Two

Mary wondered for a moment if she'd fallen asleep and was, God forbid, snoring. Every once in awhile NRR got a client who was so dull one or all of the partners would actually find themselves nodding off while discussing contracts.

Today it was Mary's turn to down a third cup of coffee and pry her eyes open with toothpicks. She shifted in her chair and focused on Ivan Garrison, a new client who had hired her to design a menu for a party he was throwing aboard his yacht, *Clara Belle*. For the past thirty minutes the forty-year-old wannabe boat captain had been sorrowfully telling Mary that he'd named the boat in honor of his dead wife, who he'd married for her "outstanding boating skill and formidable rack."

It had taken Mary a good thirty seconds to realize that Ivan was referring to his wife's chest and another ten seconds to contemplate passing him on to Olivia, since the job mainly consisted of culinary planning. But he was one of those trust-fund jerks who made Olivia's skin crawl, and the risk of having her abide by NRR's seventh vow, Do No Harm might be asking too much.

Who knew? If he took Olivia for a ride in his yellow Lamborghini and insisted she call him Captain like he did everyone else, Olivia just might bop him on the head the night before the party and serve him to his guests with an apple in his mouth the next day.

"The date for the regatta gala as you know is the twenty-fifth," he said, touching the brim of the snow-white captain's hat he had worn to both meetings. "I'll have my secretary send over the guest list. Please make sure to refer to me as Captain on the invitation. That's how my friends and business associates know me."

Aye aye, sir! Mary nodded. "Of course."

"I'd like to really pack this party. We always get enough entrants for the race, but the galas aren't as well attended."

"We could make it as a charity event," Mary suggested.

"I'll think about that." He leaned back in his chair and sighed. "Now, have I told you how I came to be called Captain?"

"No." If Ivan was going to come around every week, she'd have to invest in some NoDoz.

"As you know, it's not my given name," he said. "When I was six—wait, no, closer to eight, my nanny, her name was Alisia and she was the one who bathed me—"

"Excuse me. I'm sorry to interrupt."

Mary glanced up and smiled thankfully at her partner. "No problem, Olivia. We were just finishing up here."

Olivia acknowledged Ivan with a quick nod. "Hello, Captain." Then she turned back to Mary. "Your next client is here."

"I don't have—" Mary stopped herself. What the heck was she doing? Her savior, Olivia had clearly noticed her drooping eyelids and coffee-stained teeth, maybe even heard the beginning of the creepy nanny-and-the-eight-year-old's-bath story and was giving her a way out.

"We can discuss the rest on the phone, Captain," Mary said, standing and shaking his hand. "Or if you'd prefer, we could e-mail."

The captain sighed wistfully. "My Clara Belle loved the e-mail. Did I tell you she had twelve computers, one for every bathroom? She wanted to stay connected. I haven't had the heart to remove them."

After one more minute of commiserating about the impracticality of expensive technology in damp places, Mary told Ivan where to find the little captain's room and walked toward the lobby with Olivia.

Mary released a weary sigh. "Thank you so much."

"For what?" Olivia asked.

"The 'your next client is here' save. I'm thankful for the business, but sadly Ivan is only eccentric and strange in an uninteresting way. There's nothing worse."

Olivia looked confused. "Mary, I'm always happy to help with tedious clients, but in this case, you really do have someone waiting." She nodded toward the man sitting in one of the lobby's artfully distressed brown leather chairs.

Mary's breath caught at the sight of him, and she wanted to kick herself for the girlish reaction, but she walked toward him instead. Ethan Curtis wasn't the kind of handsome you'd see on the pages of a *Businessman Weekly*. No three-piece suits or slicked-back hair, no calm, refined demeanor. He looked edgy and ready to pounce, his severe blue eyes alert and ready for a battle. Dressed in tailored pants and an expensive, perfectly cut black shirt, his large frame ate up the leather chair as around them the air crackled with a potent mixture of desire and conflict.

"We didn't have an appointment today, Mr. Curtis," Mary said in a gently caustic tone.

Amusement flashed in his eyes. "Yes, I know. But this is urgent."

Obviously she wasn't getting rid of him anytime soon. "Let's go into my office."

"No. I need to take you somewhere."

"Impossible," she told him sharply.

"Nothing's impossible."

"I can't." Didn't he see that Olivia was still lurking around? If she overheard them, she'd get the wrong idea…well, the right idea, and Mary didn't want that. "I have insane amounts of work—"

"This is work."

Mary pressed her lips together in frustration. She felt caught in a trap. If she refused, made even the smallest of scenes, Olivia would be out here, wondering what was up. That could bring Tess, too. She eyed Ethan skeptically, lowered her voice. "You say this is work?"

"Of course." He spoke the right words, but he stared at her mouth while he said them.

"Better be." She tossed him a severe gaze before heading into her office for her purse.

Mary stepped into the world of trendy layettes and custom chintz toddler chairs and felt her heart sink into her shoes. It was the last place in the world she wanted to be. The fact that not only was she lying about being pregnant but that it would be a long, long time before she came into this type of store for any real purpose weighed on her like an anchor. She eyed the blue and pink bookcases and dressers with cute custom airplane and unicorn knobs.

"This is a baby shop, Mr. Curtis," she said quietly, sidestepping a beautiful whitewashed Morigeau-Lepine changing table.

Ethan dropped into a pale-green gliding chair. "Can we drop the 'mister'?"

"I don't think so."

He raised one brow in a mocking slant and whispered, "Hey, I've seen that tiny raspberry birthmark right below your navel."

A wash of heat slipped over her skin and she could only mutter, "Right…"

"Come sit down." He motioned for her to take the yellow duckie glider beside him. "You never seem to get off your feet."

"I'm fine. I'll stand."

"Ethan."

"Fine. Ethan," she ground out. "Now, are you going to tell me why we're in a baby shop?"

He picked up a lovely piece of original artwork from a nearby table and studied the drawing of two frogs sailing a boat. "I'm thinking we could add one more item to your workload."

"Like?"

"A nursery in my house."

Mary's pulse escalated to a frenetic pace. "You want me to design a nursery for the…our…"

"Baby, yes. I may have unlimited resources, but you weren't far off when you suggested I grew up under a rock. It was a trailer park actually. Dark, dirty and decorated with the curbside castoffs of the rich people on the other side of town. So, I have zero taste. And as you can see, I'm a guy."

She stared at him, not sure how to feel about what he'd just revealed to her. She hadn't meant to insult him with the "rock" comment. Well, maybe she had a little, but now she felt pretty damn snobby. Although, his need to be accepted by the Minneapolis bluebloods, have a child with one, made way more sense now. Not that his actions were in any way forgiven. "Look, I'm sorry about what I said…the rock thing—"

He waved away her apology with his hand, his jaw a little too tight. "It's not important. What is important however is that my child has a place to sleep. So? Is this agreeable to you?"

This wasn't a bizarre request for an NRR client. She'd designed over twenty nurseries and children's rooms over the past five years. Single fathers, gay fathers who had to admit they had no taste, even busy moms on occasion.

"I thought you might enjoy this," Ethan said, coming to his feet.

"Did you?" He wanted her to decorate her own child's room. A child that didn't exist.

She turned away from Ethan and closed her eyes, took a deep breath. What was she thinking? What was she thinking lying to someone about something so important, something as sacred as having a baby? This was getting out of hand. Yes, she'd had to protect her father, and now that he was out of danger, wasn't it time to tell Ethan Curtis that he was not going to be a daddy, suffer his censure, his threats, and get on with her life?

Fear darted into her gut. But what if he refiled charges? That was entirely possible—maybe even probable given how angry and spiteful he'd be if he learned the truth. Her father couldn't survive another arrest. No, there was no way she was allowing that to happen.

Mary fingered a swatch of green gingham fabric. It would work wonderfully for a boy or a girl. Tears sat behind her throat. She wasn't the most maternal person in the world, but she wanted a child. Someday. With a man who loved her…

"Mary?"

She turned and looked at Ethan. "Okay."

"Hello, there." A very perky blond sales clerk appeared before them, her round brown eyes wide with excitement. "So, when's our baby due?"

Before Mary could even open her mouth to say that they were just looking around, Ethan chimed in with "Early to mid April."

Mary's head whipped around so fast she wondered if she'd given herself whiplash.

Ethan shrugged. "I did the calculations."

"A spring baby," the salesgirl said, beaming at Ethan as though he were a candidate for father of the year already. "How about we start with a crib?"

Ethan gestured to Mary. "The lady's in charge."

The girl looked expectantly at Mary. "Traditional? Round? Any thoughts?"

"No thoughts," Mary said, feeling weak all of a sudden. "Not today."

The girl looked sympathetic and lowered her voice. "Mom's tired."

You have no idea, lady.

"I tried to get her to sit down," Ethan said with a frustrated shake of the head.

The girl nodded as if to say, I've seen many a pregnant woman and understood their moods. "We can do this another day."

Mary nodded. "Another day is good." Another year might be good to.

Ethan checked his watch. "It's after one." He eyed Mary with a concerned frown. "Have you eaten lunch?"

Mary shook her head. "Not yet, but I'll get something back at the office—"

"You need to eat now. You wait here. I'll go get the car."

"I have my car," she said, but he was already halfway out the door.

To make matters worse, the salesgirl sidled up to Mary, clasped her hands together and sighed. "You're so lucky."

"Why?"

She looked at Mary as though she was crazy or just plain mean. "That man is going to make a great daddy."

"If he can stop ordering people around long enough," Mary muttered to herself.

"Excuse me?"

Mary smiled at the girl, shook her head, then followed Ethan out the door.

"You know, there was an iffy-looking Thai place next to that baby store," Mary said, sipping lemonade and munching on perfectly tender chicken picata and fresh spinach salad.

Across from her, Ethan waved his fork. "This is better."

Mary shrugged, a trace of a smile in her voice. "Well, sure, if you like quiet, great food and a killer view."

Under the guise of work, Ethan had taken her to his home for some lunch. Worn-out from the experience at the baby shop, and more than a little bit curious about what kind of home a man like this one would choose, she hadn't put up much of a fuss. And her curiosity was well rewarded.

She had expected Ethan's home to mirror his office—glass and chrome and modern—but maybe she should've taken a clue from his rooftop garden instead.

There was absolutely nothing modern about the estate. It was enchanting and secluded, complete with a charming wooded drive that led straight up to the massive French-country style home.

Inside was nothing less than spectacular, but not in a showy, uptight way. Though it was sparsely furnished, the rooms were warm and rustic with lots of brick and hardwood.

Mary sipped her lemonade, taking in the soft summer afternoon on the sprawling deck that nestled right up to the edge of a private lake.

"I thought you should see the space you'll be working with," Ethan said, finishing off his last bite of chicken.

Mary nodded. "You're nothing if not helpful, Mr. Curtis."

A breeze kicked up around them, sending pre-autumn leaves swirling over the edge of the deck into the water.

"Hey, I thought we talked about this back at the baby shop. You were going to call me Ethan—"

"I only agreed to that to get you to stop talking."

"What?" he said, chuckling.

"You were bringing up the past and I wasn't interested in going there."

"The very recent past."

She attempted to look confused. "Was it? Feels like ages ago, like it didn't happen at all."

He glared at her belly. "Oh, it happened, Mary."

Heat flooded her skin, but she forced her expression to remain impassive.

His gaze found hers again and he studied her. "You've got quite an attitude on you."

"With you, yes."

"I'm sure I'm not the only one," he said, one brow raised sardonically.

"Don't you have a room to show me?"

He sighed. "Come on, Mary, can we make peace here? Maybe even start again? Friends?"

Inside the confines of his office, where she could remember who and what he was, Mary felt safe. She had her walls up, double thick. Even on his rooftop or at the baby shop, he still seemed arrogant and ever the dictator. But here, in his home, with nature and softness surrounding him, it was different. His skin seemed bronze and highly touchable, his eyes glistened like two inviting lakes beckoning her to jump in, and his clothes seemed highly unnecessary. Mary felt her defenses slipping. Forget being friends; she wanted him to kiss her again— just once so she could prove to herself that it wasn't as good as she remembered. Sure, he had more depth than he let on, but she could make no mistake about it— Ethan Curtis was a selfish, misguided man, who was solely out for himself.

She put down her napkin and tried not to stare at the lush curve of his lower lip. "I won't pretend that we're friends, or even friendly."

"Fine, but can you really despise me? For wanting a child?"

She laughed, shocked at how obtuse he was being. "Is that a serious question? Of course it's understandable and wonderful to want a child—blackmailing a woman you know nothing about to get one is not."

He leaned forward and with a trace of a growl said, "True."

"You have no excuse for your behavior?"

"None whatsoever."

They stared at each other in stubborn silence, sparks of heat, of desire, flickering between them.

Finally Ethan spoke, "Let's go see the room."

They walked side by side through the house and up the curving staircase to the second floor. Ethan had run these stairs a hundred times, alone of course. He hadn't invited many people to his home, and the ones that had made it past the foyer had never been allowed upstairs. He normally took women back to their place after a date. Less complicated that way.

These upcoming parties were going to be the first time he'd invited a large group to his home, and the thought alarmed him somewhat, though he knew it was the right business decision. If a person was going to switch insurance companies for their billion-dollar business, they would want to see the man who'd be taking it over in his natural habitat—simple as that.

"I chose the room next to mine," Ethan explained as they walked down the long hallway. "If he or she needs me in the middle of the night…" He paused at the door to the nursery and looked at her. "That's how it goes, right? They wake up at night and you go to them?"

"I wouldn't know." Her skin had taken on a grayish

pallor as she stared into the empty room with its beamed ceilings and white walls.

"Your womanly instincts must tell you something—" Ethan began, but was quickly cut off by Mary's soft laughter. "All right, I'm a little nervous about this whole thing. I want a child more than anything, but I know absolutely nothing."

"You'll get help."

"I don't do therapists."

She released a heavy sigh and turned to face him. "No, Ethan. Not that kind of help."

"What? Like a nanny or something?"

"Or something."

He shook his head. "All this child will need is me."

"Two seconds ago you were saying you didn't know a thing."

"I'll learn."

"Maybe you won't be able to give a child everything. I mean…"

"What? What do you mean?"

She gritted her teeth. "Well, you were just talking about womanly instincts. I mean, don't you think that a child needs a mother?"

Ethan felt his whole body go numb at her query and tried to shake it off, but the more he tried to control the feeling, the anger building inside him, the harder it attacked him. He heard himself mutter a scornful sound, then say, "Not from what I've noticed."

Mary's face was impassive, except for the frown lines between her brows. "What have you noticed?"

His head was swimming, his thoughts as jumpy as his skin. But why, dammit? Why was he reacting this way? The truth was he'd done just fine after his mom ran off. Sure he got into trouble with the law, but he'd gotten a hold of himself, and look at where he was today—no thanks to a mother. No, he and his kid would do just fine.

Mary felt the conflict start deep in her gut. She didn't want to give a damn about Ethan or his past or his feelings on his family, but the stark pain etched on his face was very telling and intriguing. She would never have imagined seeing the hint of a suffering boy behind the overconfident glare of the man. "Ethan," she began softly. "I'm not going to push you on this, but—"

Turning away from her, he lifted his chin and stared into the nursery. He was not about to discuss his past with her. "What do you think of the room?"

"It's great," she said in a soft voice. "Perfect. Any kid's dream."

"I'd like to get started on it right away."

"Sure."

He looked down at her once again, his eyes so dark blue and impassioned she felt her breath catch. "Mary?"

"Yes?"

"Would you mind…" He broke off, shook his head.

"What?"

"Can I touch you?"

Her self-control, always to be counted on, melted like the last bits of snow on a warm spring day. "We agreed—"

"No." He moved closer, until they were nearly touching. "Your stomach."

"Oh."

He cursed darkly. "I know it's ridiculous. Way too early. All of that. But, I…"

Her gaze dropped to her belly. "It is early."

"I know, but I just…" His mouth was close to her ear, that sensual, cynical mouth.

"All right," she heard herself utter foolishly.

Mary closed her eyes, afraid of what she might say or do when his hand gently cupped her stomach. Heat surged through the light cotton fabric of her shirt, and she was flooded with emotions. There was no child here, yet there was an ache so intense she thought she'd collapse if he didn't move his hand up toward her breasts or down between her thighs. Frustrated weakness overtook her and she wobbled against him.

"Are you all right?" he asked, holding her steady.

She had never run from anything in her life, but at that moment she had to get out of his house, away from that room, far from him. "I have to get back to the office."

"I'll drive you back."

She ignored the concern in his voice and pushed away from him. "I followed you over here, remember?"

"Maybe you should sit down for a minute. You seem—"

"The first party is Friday, correct?" she said, running her fingers through her hair, as if that would help quiet her shaking body. "If you can send me the guest list."

"Of course." He attempted to touch her again, but she moved away.

"Thank you for lunch, Ethan." Brushing past him, she walked quickly down the hallway, down the stairs and out the front door, only remembering to breathe once she was safely inside her car.

Three

"What's Olivia making?" Mary asked when she returned to the office later that day. Even in her sorry mental state, the scent she'd encountered when entering the lobby of their office building five minutes ago had made her taste buds come alive. Mouthwatering aromas wafting through their building weren't an unusual occurrence during the week, they just made her want to run up the four flights of stairs to get to the source instead of taking the very slow elevator.

Poised at the front desk, with a full plate of beautifully arranged golden spheres, Tess tried to smile. Unfortunately, her mouth was full and she could only manage a chipmunk-like grin. "Scones," she said on a sigh, pointing at the plate. "Cranberry. Have one."

"I've actually just come back from lunch, so I'm pretty stuffed."

"Seriously? Too full for one of these?"

Tess rolled her eyes, then grabbed one. "Devil."

"Don't blame the addict, kid," Tess replied, reaching for another. "Blame her supplier."

"Where is Olivia?"

"Trying out another scone recipe. Chocolate this time."

"Great."

"She has a high tea to plan. That angry groom wants something beautiful and classic to celebrate the loss of his fiancée."

"How strange, yet lovely."

"He has over sixty guests."

"Lovely for us, too, then."

Tess laughed. "So, where were you?"

Obviously Olivia hadn't told her about Ethan.

"That new client Olivia was telling me about?"

Or not. Mary glanced through the mail on the desk. "Yes. Ethan Curtis. CEO of Harrington Corp. and old-money wannabe."

"Harrington Corp.? Isn't that your family's insurance company."

Mary nodded. "Was. Before Ethan Curtis took it over."

"Interesting that he'd hire you," Tess said nonchalantly, taking another scone, but only fiddling with it on her plate.

"I've got the blue-blood background he's looking for," Mary explained. "In many respects.

"Olivia said he was pretty good-looking."

"I suppose he is."

"A clean-shaven Colin Farrell with the body of a construction worker, is what she said, I think."

"That's incredibly specific. She saw him for like five seconds."

"Just be careful," Tess said, her tone serious.

Such a strong warning from a woman who rarely got involved in the personal matters of her partners made Mary's defenses perk up. "He's just a client, Tess."

"Of course. Sure. But you know, it's always better to be safe, kid. Expect an agenda and you won't get hurt." She picked up her scone and pointed it at Mary. "You never know the true character of a person or what they're really after."

Whenever Tess spoke in this cryptic way, Mary had the burning desire to ask her what she meant by it, and maybe where the cynicism was coming from. But the women of NRR kept their pasts in the past. As for Tess's concern over Ethan Curtis's character, Mary wasn't flying blind—she knew exactly who he was and what he wanted. But her partner's advice was sound. After what had happened today, how she'd felt standing so close to him, as though she were frozen solid and he was a very inviting campfire, she had to be careful—adopt the all-business facade she normally wore with such ease and comfort.

"I'll watch my back." She tossed her partner a reassuring grin. "But in the meantime, Mr. Curtis has given me five days to plan a very swanky event. I'd better get on it." She paused over the plate of scones. "Damn that Olivia," she grumbled, grabbing one and heading toward her office.

* * *

In the past Ethan had used a local catering company for his parties. A boutique-type place, very upscale and guaranteed to impress. Their food had always been good, though at times unrecognizable. But, in his opinion, the menu and service had always felt cold and impersonal, not really his speed. For years he'd gone along with the very fancy, tasteless hors d'oeuvres, prickly flower arrangements and silent waitstaff because, well, he'd been to several events with just that type of vibe and everyone had seemed to enjoy themselves.

Then he'd asked Mary Kelley to plan his event.

When she'd come to him with the menu and details of what she had planned, he'd worried. Would his stuffy clientele appreciate her vision?

Ethan glanced around his home. Clearly, he'd worried for no reason. In five short days she'd transformed the entire first floor of his home into a relaxed, candlelit lounge, and outside on his deck and lawn, she'd created a beautiful Asian garden. It was anything but showy. In fact, the feel of the whole party was classic and elegant and totally comfortable. Smiling, helpful waitstaff milled about with delicious alcoholic concoctions like wet-cucumber and ginger-passionfruit margaritas, and Asian-French treats like miso-braised short ribs, coriander-crusted ahi tuna and Vietnamese sweet-potato fries with a chili cream dipping sauce.

Surrounded by several clients and potential clients, Ethan felt in his element and ready to do business, but he couldn't stop himself from wondering where Mary was. Earlier in the night she'd slipped away to change and reappeared right before the first doorbell chime.

Ethan had been having a difficult time keeping his eyes off her since. His gaze scanned the crowd and found her chatting with two couples, looking at ease and incredibly sexy. Her makeup was smoky and sophisticated, and she'd slicked her blond hair back into a very chic ponytail. But it was the clothes she was wearing that really made his entire body jolt. She looked as though she'd just stepped off a runway in New York. The black crisscross halter top and white pencil skirt showed off her long, slim figure to perfection. Soon she wouldn't be able to wear clothes like this, he mused thoughtfully. Her body would grow with their child, blossom with curves.

He continued to watch her as she gestured to one of the waitstaff carrying those very popular pale-green wet-cucumber margaritas. After serving the couple, Mary made her way over to Ethan and his insurance friends, her light-blue cat eyes bright with success and confidence. "Good evening. Is everyone enjoying themselves?"

The people around Ethan nodded and offered their host and hostess several enthusiastic compliments, then chuckled with amusement when Ethan declared he had to have what appeared to be the last piece of ahi and he was going to seek it out. Feeling oddly possessive in the large crowd of married and single men, Ethan led Mary out on the deck, where guests were waiting for a boat ride around the small lake.

"You haven't said anything about—" she gestured around the room "—all of this."

"Looks good," he said distractedly. The light out on the deck was even more intimate than the candles inside the house. Her neck looked soft and white and he played with the thought of leaning in and kissing her, right where her pulse thrummed gently.

"Looks good?" she repeated. "Is that all I'm going to get from you?"

"Nice choice of words," Ethan muttered, closing the gap between them so they were nearly touching, his chest to the tips of her breasts. Heat surged through Ethan's blood, and Mary must've seen the desire in his eyes because she quickly restated her question.

"What I meant was, is everything satisfactory?"

Ten feet away, around the side of the house, there was an alcove, just dark enough for them not to be spotted. He wanted to take her there, watch her pale-blue eyes turn smoky as he removed her skirt. "The food is amazing, the house looks perfect...yes, all satisfactory."

"Good."

"Great party, Curtis. Really top-notch." Downing a plate of short ribs as though they were going out of style, Ed Grasner, one of Ethan's biggest clients, walked by, no doubt headed for the boats and his wife.

Like a brick to the head, Ethan remembered why his guests were here. It was not to facilitate a seduction— he could do that on his own time. He turned back to Mary, his game face on. "The success of this evening isn't based on how much everyone eats and drinks or how great the house looks, it's based on acquiring several new clients."

Mary looked confused, as though she was watching a chameleon change colors. "Of course."

Ethan nodded toward a couple in their late thirties, sitting at one of the candlelit tables by the water. "Isaac and Emily Underwood. The St.Paul Underwoods. Very old money."

"Yes, I've heard of them."

"They own twenty-five exclusive inns around the Midwest. Get to them, get to the rest of their family. Can your efforts tonight reel in prize fish like that?"

"Is this a business party or the hunting and gaming channel?"

"I want what I want. And ninety-nine percent of the time I get it."

She shook her head at him.

He raised a brow. "I sound arrogant?"

"Arrogant, presumptuous, lacking in finesse."

Her derogatory adjectives caused him to stiffen. "Do you ever not say what's on your mind?"

"Once or twice. But it's a rarity."

Ethan had never been spoken to like this. At least not in the past fifteen years. He wasn't used to it, but for some reason with her, it didn't bother him all that much. In fact, her honesty and candor appealed to him.

"Mr. Curtis?" The pair that Ethan had just been talking about were walking toward him. The Underwoods were a handsome couple, very blond and tanned. Understated wealth oozed from them. They also appeared very much in love, their hands tightly clasped, only releasing each other when Ethan and Mary reached out a hand to greet them.

Emily gave Mary a warm, beautifully white smile. "I hear that you are the one responsible for this party?"

"I am," Mary said pleasantly. "Are you enjoying yourself this evening, Mrs. Underwood?"

The woman looked confused. "Have we been introduced?"

"Not yet. But I've heard much about you and your husband, and of course your lovely inns, from my grandparents."

"Your grandparents?"

"The Harringtons."

The casual warmth from a moment ago morphed into a look of understanding and respect. "Of course. I should have noticed it before. You have your grandmother's eyes. The shape."

Mary smiled, but her stomach churned lightly as it did whenever someone found a similarity between her and her grandmother. She didn't despise the woman like her father did, but growing up she had always been compared with her and had desperately wanted to be compared to her mother instead. But they'd looked so different it was almost impossible to see.

Ethan's hand came to rest on her back and she instinctively leaned into him. "Have you had a boat ride?" he asked, gesturing toward the lake. When they nodded, he asked them if they'd tried the food.

Chuckling, Isaac spoke then, "The food is amazing,

Curtis. Really. Both Emily and I have taken full advantage of your hospitality." He turned to Mary. "We must have the name of your chef. There are a few things we'd love to add to our menus."

"Of course," Mary replied. "The chef is my business partner, Olivia. I'll make sure to give you her name and number before you leave. But first, I see that the waitstaff are bringing out the desserts. You must try the pistachio crème brûlée with orange ice cream."

"Sounds delicious," Emily said with childlike enthusiasm.

Lowering her voice, Mary said conspiratorially, "Heavenly actually." She gestured toward the house. "Let's make sure you both have at least one."

Emily giggled. "At least. Come along, Isaac."

Before Mary could disappear, Ethan grabbed her arm. "Why are you sending them away? I wanted to speak with them about—"

"Relax, Curtis," she said softly, her eyes bright with mischief. "They'll be back. And because they want to, not because they've been hooked, yanked onto a boat and gutted."

Equally shocked and impressed, Ethan studied her. "Very nice."

She inclined her head. "Thank you."

Ethan's gaze followed her hungrily as she walked off to feed crème brûlée to his guests.

Some men resembled excessively tall penguins in their tuxedoes. Some looked awkward and uncomfortable. But Ethan Curtis wore his like a second skin. As he stalked his estate, he looked like a predator in search of his next prey—and he seemed to take his targets down with amazing speed and assuredness. By the end of the night, several potential clients had verbally signed on to Harrington Corp.'s already thick roster, and as Mary had predicted, the Underwoods had come back to him in a sugar haze, asking for a meeting at his office the following Monday.

When Mary found Ethan he was in the kitchen, looking very pleased with himself, his bow tie undone and falling against his open white shirt. Beer in hand, he chatted with the on-site chef, Jean Paul, as the man prepared to leave.

Mary shut her eyes against the sudden and unbidden image of Ethan out of that tux, his heavily muscled, tanned skin pressing down into the cushion of a woman's body—her body. She despised her reaction to him and to the memory of those nights together. Why couldn't she get it through her thick skull that those moments were over? Yes, sometimes he looked at her with a flicker of desire in his eyes, but the moment was over in seconds and he was back to business. He hadn't even commented on how she looked tonight, and she was really working it.

She grabbed her purse from the counter by the fridge. What did it matter? She was the one insisting that nothing romantic ever happen again. She faced him and spoke in her most professional voice. "Well, we're done here. If there's nothing else…"

Jean Paul discreetly returned to his knives, and Ethan regarded her with open respect. "I owe you a very big thank-you."

"You're welcome. It was a success, I think."

"Completely." He came to stand before her, his dark-blue eyes glittering with the satisfaction of a tiger who'd just bagged several hunters for dinner. His sensuous mouth turned up at the corners as he grinned at her, stealing her breath. "In fact, many of my guests are wondering what you'll come up with next."

"They'll just have to wait and see."

"I'm wondering, too." One of his dark brows lifted. "Do I have to wait?"

If he came any closer, she was going to lose it. Feeling irritatingly light-headed, she reached out for the granite countertop to steady herself. "We could discuss the menus and themes at any time."

"How about now? I didn't get one of the boat rides."

"I don't know if the guys are still out there."

His grinned widened. "I think I can manage to take you for a ride myself."

"Ethan Curtis, where have you been?" The slow, whiskey-smooth female voice came from behind Mary, and she turned with a jerk to see a five-foot-nine Playboy playmate, dressed in an orange tank dress.

"Allison, where did you come from?" Ethan asked, sounding more annoyed than surprised.

"Didn't you say eleven? I don't wear a watch, but I could swear I'm right on time." Her voice and body language just screamed sex.

Mary heard Ethan curse, but she didn't dare turn back to face him, not with her neck turning red as she knew it was. He had a date. An after-party date. Of course he did. Why not?

"Wait for me by the pool, Allison," Ethan said, his voice soft but commanding. "I'm not quite finished here."

Finding her nerve at long last, Mary forgot about her red neck and gave the hot blonde a hotter glare. "Allison, is it?"

She smiled. "Two Ls and two Ns."

Brilliant and beautiful, Mary mused dryly. What a combination. "You don't need to go anywhere. Mr. Curtis and I are finished." She turned to Ethan and gave him a fake smile. "I'll call you in a few days, sir—to discuss the next function."

Anger burned in her stomach and, as she walked swiftly through his house and out the front door, she called herself fourteen kinds of fool for even considering him in a romantic way. He was an egotistical, spoiled player who had no idea what he really wanted.

"Mary, slow down." Ethan caught up with her on his driveway and grabbed her hand as she tried to open her car door.

She brushed him off. "I have work waiting for me at home and you have a Barbie twin waiting for you by the pool."

"I made that date weeks ago. Before…well…" He pushed a hand through his hair. "This is awkward."

"Damn right," she retorted in a sharp voice. "So, I'm going to go now before it gets any more awkward."

"No."

"I'm not into threesomes, Curtis."

"I didn't even know you were interested in a twosome."

Gritting her teeth, Mary stared at him. "Ditto."

He took a moment to process her meaning. "If you think I don't want to go to bed with you again, you're wrong."

"Who the hell could tell?"

"What does that mean?"

"You hardly looked at me tonight," she said with a scowl. "Then the cover of *Sluts-R-Us* magazine walks in and your eyes pop out of—"

"I see you, Mary," he interrupted hotly. "I remember every damn detail."

"But?"

"Weren't you the one who said that what happened those nights at the lake would never happen again?"

She hated when the truth was tossed in her face. "Yes." She wrenched open her car door.

"And it's complicated, isn't it?" he continued. "What we did? What we made? Who I am."

"Who you are? I can't figure it out."

"The bastard who blackmailed you…basically."

His words shocked her. The easy admission of something so base and vile. She got in her car and slammed the door. "So, what? You feel guilty?"

"No."

"Of course not. You see nothing wrong with what you did."

"I don't feel guilty, that's true. But I do feel…" He

cursed. "Conflicted. Protective." He shrugged, as if the truth surprised the hell out of him. "Isn't that the damnedest thing?"

"Protective? Of whom?"

"You."

"You're protecting me from you?"

"Maybe. I don't know."

"Well, stop it," she said caustically, gunning her engine. "Sex doesn't have to be any more emotionally significant than a really charged football game."

The words exploded into the air like fireworks, but she didn't believe them, and she knew that he knew she didn't believe it. What was she trying to do? Why couldn't she abandon this idea of him and her, one more time, or two or three? What was she? A masochist?

"Mary—"

"Go prove my point to Allison in there," she said bitingly before shoving the car into Reverse and taking off down the quiet, wooded drive.

Four

Mary sat in Little Bo and Peep's baby shop, up to her eyeballs in terry cloth, stretch cotton, bouncy seats and black and white mobiles. For the past twenty minutes, she hadn't been able to pick out a single thing for the nursery. She knew exactly what clothes she loved, what crib and bassinet she wanted, she even knew the drawer pulls she would pick out if this were all real. But designing a nursery for a child that didn't exist was next to impossible. She felt like a total fraud and she wanted to give up.

The doorbell over the shop entrance jangled merrily, and Mary watched a young couple come through the door with excited grins. They oohed and aahed as they moved from one quaint set of nursery furniture set to the next, hands clasped tightly, the woman's round stomach looking like a sweet watermelon. She wanted that. A real relationship, a real baby…something impossible to have with Ethan Curtis. Mary's mind rolled back to the party and how it had ended. For the past two days she'd thought of nothing but him and that blonde, and her own irrational need to be with him again. She'd wondered what had happened after she'd left. Had Ethan met her by the pool? Did they go for a swim together? Allisonn—two Ls, two Ns—hadn't seemed like the kind of woman who thought swimsuits were all that important.

Beside her, the young mother pointed at a tiny Minnesota Twins baseball cap and squealed with delight, catching Mary's eye in the process. Mary forced a smile, then moved on to look at bathtubs and safety accessories. Why the hell did she care what Ethan did? Or *who* he did, for that matter? She had to get over this.

The saleswoman walked by her again with that look all salespeople give a person when they think you're lingering without purpose.

Are you stealing or just indecisive?

"Right, I get it," Mary grumbled under her breath as she abandoned the bath supplies and headed to the front of the store. Nothing was going to happen today. She wasn't about to do any work on the nursery in her state of mind. If Ethan asked her how she was progressing, she'd just have to stall and—

"Mary?"

Coming into the shop just as Mary was exiting was a very elegant woman in her midseventies, dressed in a thin crepe navy blue suit, her white hair swept off her mildly wrinkled face in a tightly pinned chignon.

"Grandmother? What are you doing here?"

Grace Harrington surveyed her granddaughter, her perfectly arched brows lifting at the sight of Mary's plain black pantsuit and slightly scuffed heels. To Grace Harrington, clothes were like Ziplock baggies, only good for one use.

"Pearl Edicott's granddaughter is expecting twins," her grandmother said in a pinched tone. "Pearl has the most horrific taste. It's a very good thing she knows it."

"Very good thing," Mary repeated, smiling in spite of herself. Grace Harrington was an over-the-top snob, and if Mary had any sense, she'd probably detest her. After all, Grace wasn't all that warm either, more days than not she found something wrong with Mary's clothing or hairstyle, and she treated her help like they didn't breathe the same air as she did. And then there was the fact that she had cut Mary's mother out of her life when she'd married Hugh.

Yet, with all of that, Mary felt a connection with her, a strange admiration that went far beyond her wealth. Grace was smart, well-read and a stickler for speaking her mind. Mary could really respect that. She and her grandparents were rarely *simpatico*, but they were her blood, and had always wanted to be a part of her life, and strangely Mary's mother had never discouraged her from seeing them.

Grace picked up two twin chenille baby robes that cost a hundred dollars each and eyed them closely. "And what are you doing here, my dear?"

"Designing a nursery for a client."

"Ah, yes, your business. How is that going?"

"Great."

Grace forgot about the robes for a moment and focused on Mary, her lips pursed. "This isn't for one of those two-father homes, is it?"

"Not this time."

"A couple, then?" She didn't give Mary a chance to answer as she clucked her tongue disapprovingly. "A mother who doesn't want to create her own child's room. How modern."

Mary was about to ask her grandmother if she herself had actually designed her own daughter's nursery or if she'd hired three or four interior designers to make it happen, but she knew she'd probably get an answer that resembled something like, "It was my vision. As usual, the help was only there to execute it."

"The nursery is for a single father actually," Mary told her.

"Anyone I know?"

Mary's brow lifted. "Now how many single fathers do you socialize with, Grandmother?"

Grace gave her a blank look. "None…that I know of." Spotting a beautiful pink-and-blue blanket draped over one of the handcrafted armchairs, Grace turned her back on Mary. "Well, this chenille is lovely. It reminds me of the very one your mother carried around for years. If the maid even spoke of washing it, she would…" Grace stopped abruptly and cleared her throat.

Mary was grateful not to have to see the woman's

face in that moment. Turning toward a row of onesies, she quickly changed the subject. "Babies are really no bigger than dolls, are they?"

"For a short time, yes," Grace replied softly. "But before you even realize it they are grown and deciding what they will wear and who they will marry without any input from you."

"There you are." A booming male voice broke through all the femininity. "I called your office and Olivia said you'd be—"

"Ethan?" In the heaviness of her conversation with Grace, Mary hadn't heard the bell over the door. If she had heard—and seen—who was about to enter the shop, she would've been out the door in a matter of seconds. This was not good.

Ethan spotted Grace and changed instantly from casual guy to cynical business mogul. "Mrs. Harrington. What a pleasant surprise."

"I doubt that," the older woman said dryly.

Before her grandmother could connect the single father with Ethan, Mary said quickly, "I'm organizing several functions for Mr. Curtis."

"Is that so?" Grace said, pursing her lips as if she'd just gotten a whiff of rotting fish, or as if the thought of her blue-blooded granddaughter working for the upstart who had basically stolen her family's company made her want to throw up. "When did he hire you?"

In other words, how long has this been going on and why was I not informed?

"Just a few weeks ago," Mary replied.

"And he has a meeting with you in a baby boutique?"

"No."

No doubt sensing that Mary was floundering, Ethan jumped in to save her. "We were supposed to meet at the restaurant next door, but I saw your granddaughter in here and wanted to start early. As you know, Mrs. Harrington, I have little patience and zero time. I was in the neighborhood seeing a client and there was something I needed to discuss with Miss Kelley that couldn't wait. Luckily she agreed to meet with me."

"Luckily for you she agreed to take you on as a client, Mr. Curtis," Grace said frigidly.

He nodded. "Your granddaughter is very talented."

"A fact of which I am well aware."

"Knowing that your granddaughter is planning the event, maybe you'll reconsider the brunch on Saturday."

"Perhaps," she said tightly, then turned to Mary. "I have to run, my dear."

"But the gift for the twins…"

"This shop is a little too new money for my taste, and you know how I despise that." She didn't have to look at Ethan to get her point across. "Your father is out of harm's way now, I hear."

"Yes," Mary said, surprised her grandmother would bring something like that up, much less care.

"Nasty business, that. But we were in no position to help, unfortunately." After two air kisses to Mary's cheeks and nothing whatever for Ethan, she left them.

"That woman couldn't hate me more if I spit on her shoe," Ethan muttered.

"Oh, yes she could, but I wouldn't advise trying it."

"You'd think I stole the company right out from under their noses."

"Didn't you?"

He gave her a haughty look. "Harrington Corp. was in trouble. Your grandfather was really slipping. Clients weren't getting serviced the way they had in the past and many were threatening to walk. I didn't steal anything. If anything I saved that damn company."

"Pretty much the same as stealing it, to my grandparents." Mary took her cell phone out of her pocket and showed it to him. "Now, you have my phone number, right?"

"Yes."

"Couldn't you have called me instead of tracking me down?"

"Why? Did I embarrass you?" he asked coldly.

"Don't be so thick, Curtis. I'm in a baby shop. I had to dance fast with my grandmother about why I was here, then why you were here—"

"*I* danced fast on that one," he interrupted.

She ignored him. "You know I want to keep this quiet. I thought we both did."

"I never said I wanted to keep anything quiet—"

"Hello, there." The saleswoman who had been watching Mary for the past thirty minutes in annoyance joined them, completely smiley-faced and enthusiastic at the sight of Ethan. "Daddy's here."

Ethan looked pleased with the comment and nodded. "He is."

"Would you and your wife like some lemonade before you get started?"

Mary snorted derisively and said, "I'm not his—"

"Yes, we would," Ethan said, cutting her off before following the saleswoman to a small refreshment area.

For the next twenty minutes Mary sat beside Ethan and watched as the saleswoman laid blankets and rugs, hats and booties, washtubs and soothing lullaby CDs at Ethan's feet as though he were the sultan of Bruni.

Feeling close to exploding if she stayed in the shop one more minute, Mary leaned in and whispered to Ethan, "I have to get back to the office," then grabbed her purse and headed for the door.

He caught up with her, placing his hand on her arm. "We need to talk."

"About?" she asked, trying to ignore the heat of his fingers searing into her skin.

"The brunch."

"Call my office and we'll set something up for tomorrow—"

"No, I'm the client. You can come to my office." His jaw hardened, letting her know there was no denying his command. "Today, four-thirty."

As she struggled to maintain her calm exterior, Mary fought the desire that simmered beneath. "Fine. Four-thirty."

"You look exhausted."

Not exactly the first thing a woman wants to hear

when the man she finds overwhelmingly attractive opens his office door.

"Thanks," Mary uttered sarcastically.

Ethan grinned, gestured toward the chocolate brown leather couch. "Sit down."

"I'm fine."

"We're not going to discuss the brunch while you stand. This could take a while."

"How long are you estimating?"

"Why? Do you have a date or something?"

Standing on either side of the coffee table, like two gunslingers, they stared at each other.

"Not the best joke I've made this week."

"No."

"Come on, have a seat," Ethan said, dropping onto the plush leather and grinning.

On a weary sigh, she plunked down on the couch. "Okay, I'm sitting, now let's start with the menu. I think we should go for a southern theme. Olivia has this New Mexican menu— Wait, what are you doing?"

Before Mary could stop him, Ethan had taken off her shoes and placed her feet in his lap. "I'm helping you to relax."

"Why?"

"Why not?"

"I'll tell you why not. I'm here for business not for pl—" She came to screeching halt, which made Ethan's eyes glitter even more wickedly.

"If this helps," he began. "Rubbing your aching feet is business. Technically."

"I can't wait to hear this."

"It's my job, my duty—my business, if you will. Or so I've read."

She looked surprised. "You've been reading books on…"

"Pregnancy? Yep."

"Seriously?"

He nodded. "Pregnancy, baby care, labor, postpartum, breastfeeding—"

"Okay, that's enough," she said, relaxing back into the couch as Ethan's strong hands worked the tired knots in her arches. "Five minutes max."

He laughed. "I've learned many useful things."

"Like?" she asked, trying to keep her eyes open and the soft, cozy sound out of her voice.

"Like nausea and strange cravings are very normal in the first trimester."

"Uh-huh."

"So are leg cramps and exhaustion."

"Yep."

"And an unusually high sex drive."

Her eyes flew open and she sat up, swung her legs to the floor. It took her a moment to tamp down the tremors of need running through her. She felt the urge so strongly, all she wanted him to do was continue touching her. She wanted his mouth on hers, nudging her lips apart with his tongue… "All right," she said breathlessly. "Southern food, maybe Southwest or Cajun. What about having an autumn-barn-dance theme for your brunch?"

"A heavy sex drive is nothing to be ashamed of, Mary."

She tilted her chin up. "I've never been ashamed of it."

What she was saying dawned on him almost immediately, and his eyes lit with mischief, his lips parted sensuously.

"Now, can we get back to this?" she asked coolly.

He wouldn't allow her to look away. "Nothing happened with Allisonn."

Her heart skipped and she swallowed nervously. She wanted to tell him that she couldn't care less about blondie, but he wouldn't believe her. "This doesn't sound like brunch discussion."

"Mary…" he began, his voice the husky baritone she remembered from those nights at the lake.

"Listen, Curtis, what you do in your house, bedroom, pool, etcetera is your business. Let's just get on with this."

"Why are you so hard?"

"Bad genes," she responded succinctly which made him laugh. "Not from my parents. They were angels. But they say attitude skips a generation."

Shaking his head, he stared at her for a moment, then he stood up and reached for her. "Dance with me?"

"You've got to be kidding."

"We'll make it business related. Show me what you're talking about with this barn concept. There's got to be some dancing involved on my deck, right?"

"Yes, but there's no music."

"I could turn some on, but I don't think we need it," He touched his temple with his index finger. "It's all in here."

Laughing, she took his hand and let him pull her to her feet and into his arms. "You have country music playing up there?"

He pretended to be insulted by her query. "Blues, baby. Only the blues for me."

Her toes sank into the plush carpet and she sank into Ethan's embrace. His hand gripped her waist, then slid to her back to pull her closer. She felt feminine and unsure, but she didn't want him to release her.

"I don't know how to dance," she admitted.

"I'm not that great at it, either," he said. "But I can manage a few turns and the side-to-side swaying."

His eyes were so expressive, so full of life. They could leap from anger to lust to boredom to amusement in mere moments, but it was these times that made her toes curl, the times when he stared at her with unabashed longing.

As he rocked back and forth, as his hips brushed hers and his palm pressed possessively against her hand, Mary experienced a feeling so powerful, so new it made her heart thump painfully in her chest. She was enjoying herself, with Ethan Curtis, the man who had forced her into— A man she should never enjoy herself with.

Her thoughts dropped away suddenly as Ethan quickened his pace, twirling her first to the right, then the left. With a sinful grin, he grasped both of her hands and gave her a gentle push back, then he turned her and pulled her into his body, so her back was pressed against his chest.

She glanced over her shoulder at him and smiled at the amusement in his eyes. "Tell anyone about this and I'm never dancing with you again."

Laughing with delight, Mary let him sway them both to the right and left, then squealed when he dipped her. When he rolled her out toward the couch, she released him and dropped back on the brown leather cushions. Chuckling along with her, Ethan did, too. For a moment neither of them spoke, then they both turned to look at each other.

"We'd better be careful," Ethan said.

"Why?" Mary asked breathlessly. "What do you mean?"

He reached over and brushed a strand of honey-colored hair from her cheek. "If we don't watch our step we might have fun together—or worse, actually start liking each other."

To Mary's delight, the brunch fell on a glorious late-August day. The trees were starting to contemplate change, their green leaves making room for rich golds, ruby reds and pumpkin oranges. Mary had nixed the Cajun idea, but the pre-autumn Southern barn theme was there and looking fabulous. As she meandered through the guests, who had almost doubled in size since the last party, she took in her handiwork with a proud grin. The deck and surrounding land was decorated with an odd but interesting, contemporary rustic charm; hay bales in glass troughs like funky center-pieces, scarecrows dressed like runway models, Tom Sawyer-style rafts in the water, and on and on. Then there was the food. Pumpkin and sage soup in minia-ture pumpkins, fried catfish with a spicy green tomato relish, mustard greens with pancetta, watermelon and pecan pie tartlets.

Everyone seemed relaxed, the stuffy atmosphere of this crowd's customary Saturday cocktail party forgotten. Diamonds still sparkled from ears, wrists and fingers, but the backdrop was denim and Ralph Lauren plaid.

Mary spotted five-star-inns' Isaac and Emily Underwood coming toward her and smiled welcomingly. She knew that, as of last Monday, the couple were now Ethan's clients. "Well, hello, there. Are you two enjoying yourselves?"

"Your creativity is astounding, Mary," Isaac said, gesturing to the backyard.

"Thank you."

"Yes, amazing," Emily added.

Isaac dropped his voice to a conspiratorial whisper, "Even though we don't have to work, the feeling of success can bring great rewards, don't you think?"

Mary's brows drew together. Contrary to what the Underwoods believed was reality, Mary had to work for every penny. The Harringtons didn't help her one bit, never had, nor had she ever asked them to.

"This is a great success," Emily said, two-carat diamond studs sparkling in her ears. "Especially for Ethan. Invitations to his parties will be sought-after now."

"Now?"

Heat spread across Emily's face and she stumbled to explain. "Well, what I mean to say is…"

Isaac quickly covered for her. "Curtis is brilliant,

and he has the client list to prove it, but as far as social-izing…well, he's not really one of us, you understand."

She certainly did, and she had to resist the urge to grab the pumpkin out of Isaac's hand and dump the contents over his head. Lucky for her and for them, the Underwoods spotted another group of snotty elitists over by the bar and excused themselves. Why did Ethan want to be a part of this world? she wondered, heading inside the house. She scanned the room looking for him, expecting to find him in the center of a group of wealthy people who were looking for free advice, but he wasn't there. She sidled up to one of the waitstaff. "Have you seen Mr. Curtis?"

"I think he's in the kitchen."

"Alone?"

"No, there's a full kitchen staff in there, Ms. Kelley."

"I mean, was he with anyone? A guest?" she asked tightly. Like maybe a Tiffany—one F, two Ys?

The man shook his head. "Not that I saw."

As she walked toward the kitchen, the sound of clanging pots and hustling staff was interspersed with a shrill, critical voice that Mary instantly recognized as her grandmother's.

The door opened and as a mortified-looking waitress rushed out with a plate of food, Mary heard the older woman's voice again. "You can take my family's com-pany, hire my granddaughter to act as your wife at parties and invite the top shelf as your guests, but that will never make you one of us."

Interrupting the conversation didn't sound like a

good plan. She didn't want to embarrass Ethan any further. So Mary watched through a crack in the door. The room was busy with waitstaff, chefs and to Mary's horror, not only her grandmother, but two of her grandmother's closest friends. Grace Harrington stood a few feet from Ethan, who had his back to the sleek Wolf range, her friends behind her like a scene from one of those movies about exclusive high school cliques.

"Breeding cannot be bought," Grace continued, her tone spiteful and cruel. "Where and who you come from is in every movement you make. Make no mistake about it, Mr. Curtis, you wear your trailer-park upbringing like a second skin."

The room stilled. The chefs stopped chopping, the waitstaff looked horrified as they tried to stare at anything but Ethan.

White-hot fury burned in Ethan's eyes. "I know exactly where I come from, Mrs. Harrington, and I'm proud of it."

"Is that so? Then why try so hard to impress us all?"

"My work makes enough of an impression to satisfy me. These events are a way to gain more clients. After all," he said with a slow smile, "before I came along, Harrington Corp. was not only hemorrhaging money but about to lose seventy percent of their client base as well."

Grace's jaw dropped, and she looked as though she couldn't breathe. Ditto with the geriatric sentinels behind her. Mary had never seen her grandmother bested before, and she felt oddly sorry for her, but knew the older woman had it coming to her. Grace Harrington could dish it out, and maybe now she would learn to take it.

Mary watched Ethan grab a beer from the counter and tip it toward the threesome. "Good afternoon, ladies. I have every confidence that you can find the front door from here."

And then he was coming her way, in ten seconds he'd bump right into her. Mary dropped back into a small alcove off the hallway and waited for him to leave the kitchen and pass by her. His jaw tight, his stride purposeful, he walked past her and in the opposite direction of the party. After waiting a moment for her grandmother and her friends to leave, Mary followed Ethan. She had a good idea where he'd be.

She climbed the stairs and walked down the hall, unsure of what she was going to say to him when she found him. The door to the nursery was closed, but that didn't dissuade her.

Without knocking, she entered the room. Ethan was lying on his back on the floor, staring out the enormous bay window. Sunlight splashed over his handsome face, illuminating his pensive expression.

Mary sat beside him. Maybe he'd been right that day in his office, after their musicless dance, maybe they were becoming friends. God only knew why, after their history. But the fact was she understood him a little better now, understood what drove him. Her mother had felt some of the same feelings of not being good enough, not knowing where she belonged or who really cared about her for herself and not how much money she had.

"She's right."

Ethan's words jarred her, brought her back to the present. "Who's right?"

"Your grandmother. I'm not worth much more than the trailer I was born in."

"That's not exactly what she said." Mary knew that she sounded as though she were defending Grace, when that's not what she was trying to do at all. She knew her grandmother had been cold and cruel, but Ethan could be that way as well.

"That's what she said, Mary. I've heard versions of that diatribe many times. From my ex-wife, from my own mother. Doesn't seem to matter how hard I work." He shrugged. "I'll never escape it."

"This self-pitying thing has to stop, Ethan."

He sat up, stared at her with cold eyes. "What?"

"Why do you care?" she demanded.

"What?"

"Why do you care what any of them think?"

The anger dropped away, and he shook his head. Just kept shaking his head. "I have no idea."

"Why can't you be satisfied with the life you've created?"

The double meaning wasn't lost on either of them, and in that moment, Mary knew it was just a matter of time before she confessed the truth about her pregnancy. She didn't want to care about him. He'd forced her to make some abominable decisions…and yet…

She put a hand on his shoulder, and in less than an instant he covered it with his own. "Under that layer of pride and arrogance," she said softly, "is a pretty decent guy. I can't help but believe that."

He leaned in until his forehead touched hers. "Even with everything that's happened?"

"Yes."

He tipped her chin up and with a soft groan his mouth found hers in a slow, drugging kiss. Mary opened to him, even suckled his bottom lip until he uttered her name and pulled her closer, his tongue mating with hers.

She protested when he pulled away from her, whispering a barely audible no.

With his face still so close to her own, he regarded her intently. "Are you pitying me, Mary?"

She wanted his mouth, his tongue, his skin against hers and no more questions. "Does it matter?" she uttered huskily.

A long moment of silence passed, and then Ethan groaned, a frustrated, animal-like sound. "No," he muttered, closing his eyes, nuzzling her cheek until he found her mouth again.

Five

Despite the open window, the air in the room had become stiflingly warm. Mary's limbs felt heavy, and she clung to Ethan for support. His mouth was hard on hers, his breath sweet and intoxicating. For a moment she wondered if she was drunk, but then realized she had been sipping seltzer water all morning. Mouth slanting, Ethan unleashed the full strength of his need, his tongue against hers, caressing the tip until Mary was breathless and limp. Whatever he wanted to do, she was a willing participant.

Without a word, Mary started unbuttoning her white blouse, her fingers shaking. Her skin needed to breathe, needed to be touched. As Ethan chuckled softly against her lips, she tugged away at her shirt, wishing she could just rip it off.

"Let me," he uttered hoarsely.

"And this," she practically begged, struggling with the hooks on her pale-pink bra.

"Tell me what you want, Mary."

"You."

"My weight on top of you? My chest brushing against your nipples?"

"Your mouth."

His head was in the crook of her neck, his forehead nuzzling her, his teeth nipping at her skin. "On your mouth? On your breasts? Do you want me to suckle them like I did your tongue?"

"Yes," came her ragged whisper.

Gently he pulled the straps over her shoulders, eased her bra to her waist. She felt as though she were falling, sliding down, down, until she landed against plush, fuzzy white carpet. Her back to the floor, Ethan poised on top of her, his dark blue eyes hungry, almost desperate, Mary struggled to catch her breath.

"Ethan," she rasped.

Ethan paused, his body pulsing with heat. He'd never heard her say his name like that—desperately.

His body tight to the point of pain, Ethan slid his hand up her torso to her rib cage and gently cupped one breast. Instantly hungry for more, he brushed his thumb over her nipple until it stiffened into a rosy peak. His mouth watered. He'd tasted her before, but the memory had been little comfort over the past weeks.

"You are so beautiful," he whispered, leaning forward into the warmth of her body, her skin, his mouth grazing the tender bud.

Gasping, she arched her back, her chest rising and falling rapidly, one hand fisting the carpet. Her skin was so hot, electric, and he couldn't help himself, he covered her with his mouth and suckled deeply.

"Oh…" she uttered breathlessly, cupping her other breast. "Oh, Ethan, please."

Ethan rooted between her ribs to her other breast, over her fingers until he found the sweet, taut peak in the center. Her body danced beneath his, her hips pumped as though he was inside her, and how he longed to be.

So caught up in the moment, Ethan gently sank his teeth into the pink flesh surrounding her nipple as he continued to flick the tight bud. Her breath quickened, and he could hear her heart pounding in her chest. He wanted to make her climax, just with his mouth on her breast, and she was close, so close. But then outside the window came the sounds of people laughing and talking, some loud enough to hear.

"Where do you think Curtis ran off to?" one said.

"Back to the office?" someone suggested, chuckling.

The conversation wasn't lost on Mary or Ethan, and they stilled, looked at each other, their breathing labored. Then after a moment, Mary let out a frustrated sigh and rolled away from him.

Feeling like an ass, Ethan didn't say anything as he watched her dress, but when she finally looked at him, pink-cheeked, slightly disheveled and, judging by her eyes, still on the verge of orgasm, he couldn't stop himself.

"No farther?" he asked gently.

She shook her head, deep regret in her eyes, but from what, he wasn't sure. "We have to get back to the party."

"God, why?"

"They're leaving."

"I don't care—"

"Yes, you do," she said, coming to her feet, smoothing her blouse. "We need to make an appearance, say goodbye to those who remain. You don't want people thinking that you completely disappeared."

"I don't give a damn what they think." Desire still raged through him. He wanted to play caveman and drag her off to his bed and lock the door behind him. "I want to finish this."

"Another time."

He was about to tell her that he didn't want to wait, but he knew that determined look on her face, knew better than to try to sway or push her. "I'm holding you to that," he grumbled.

By the time they returned, separately of course, to the party, most of the guests had gone. There were a few stragglers milling about, and while Mary thanked and paid the staff, Ethan showed his face to the last of the guests.

He was in his office when Mary found him a half hour later.

"Well, the general consensus is that everyone had a good time," she said.

"Everyone?" he asked pointedly, his gaze intense.

She bit her lip, which made his groin tighten painfully. "I should get going."

"Stay until the end," he said.

"This is the end. Everyone's gone, even the wait and kitchen staffs have taken off."

He sat back in his chair. "I meant stay until the end of the night…when it gets light outside and my housekeeper serves breakfast."

"Ethan…"

"You could stay upstairs in my bed. Because you want to…this time."

She sighed, let her eyes fall closed for a moment. When she opened them again, he saw the same look in her eyes as he had upstairs. She wasn't finished with him or what they'd started, but she also wasn't about to agree to stay with him, either. She shook her head. "I'm sorry." Then turned and left the room.

Her ancient Betty Boop bedside lamp clicked on and Mary uttered a tired, "Man…"

Her father's face, bed-worn and confused, stared down at her. "What are you doing here, lass?"

"Sleeping."

"Why?"

She glanced at her matching Betty Boop clock, both it and the lamp presents from her parents for her twelfth birthday. "Because it's four in the morning."

Hugh sat on the bed and dragged a hand through his rumpled hair. "Why are you here and not in your apartment?"

Right. Mary glanced around her old bedroom. Not a thing out of place since she'd found her own apartment at nineteen. Same red-checked curtains and white dresser. She smiled halfheartedly when she spotted her *Xanadu* album in the corner by the old turntable.

Her father cleared his throat, and Mary looked at him sheepishly. "All right, I ran away."

"Did you indeed?" he said, his shaggy brows lifting.

"From a boy." Actually from a man, a gorgeous, fever-inducing man, who wanted her in his bed almost as much as he wanted the nonexistent child in her belly. Mary shook her head. What a mess. She burrowed deeper under her old, white down comforter.

"You won't be telling me why you're running from this boy, will you lass?"

Her lips pressed tightly together, she shook her head like a stubborn toddler. How could she possibly? Her dad wouldn't understand what she'd done—the lengths to which she'd gone to protect him. Or worse yet, he'd understand perfectly, feel incredibly guilty and fall deeper into the chasm of despair he was already stuck in.

"You just need a bit of the old family house, do you?" he asked finally, shooing a tiny insect away from the lamp.

She gave him a grateful smile. "If you don't mind, Pop."

"You know you're always welcome here, lass." He paused for a moment, his eyes concerned. "I just don't want you to be running away from your problems too often. You'll never have time to sit down and take a breath if you do."

"I know."

"I love you, lass."

"I love you too, Pop."

When her father left the room, Mary lay back against her pillow and stared out at the same moon she'd watched change from sliver to crescent to full so many times when she was a kid. What had started out as the only foreseeable way to keep her father out of jail, or from a trial at the very least, had become a nightmare that she wanted to wake up from. She and Ethan had a meeting next week, and no matter how difficult it would be, she was not going to run away from the truth. She was going to tell him everything.

The wind off the lake whipped her hair from side to side, as though trying to make up its mind which direction to go. It was Sunday morning, a day Mary usually reserved for the newspaper, coffee and as many Danishes as she could eat without exploding, but when Ivan Garrison had called and asked her to see his boat, she'd readily accepted. The fact was, she was dying for some impersonal work to take her mind off Ethan.

After seeing his eighty-four-foot yacht, and having a quick discussion about where he'd like everything set up for the gala, the captain had asked her to take a sail on the very boat that he would be racing that day. Mary had been on very few sailboats in her time, and had been a little afraid of seasickness, but after popping a couple of Dramamine, she'd hopped aboard and found life on the water rather magnificent.

After they'd rounded the lake twice, Ivan headed back to the marina. Over the wind and the lapping of the water, Mary called, "This is great! I think your guests will be very impressed, Captain."

Ivan grinned at her. "Not just by the gala, I'm hoping."

Confused, she said, "I'm sorry?"

"I've decided to take your advice and make this a charity event."

Mary nodded. So, the captain did have a soul after all. Shocking, he wasn't just a Lamborghini-driving playboy. She'd have to tell Olivia.

"So all the entry fees will go to charity?" she called as Ivan maneuvered around in the marina, approaching the dock at a very slow speed.

"My financial advisors have told me that this will be a great tax write-off."

So he wasn't exactly Mother Teresa, but at least he had agreed to do something worthwhile. Maybe she wouldn't mention this to Olivia.

"Have you decided which charity appeals to you?" she asked him.

"Cancer's pretty popular."

"True."

Ivan slowly entered the slip, then placed the transmission in neutral and let the wind blow the boat back. "But which one to choose?" he called, securing the boat's front dock line first. "Children? Lung? Breast?"

Mary removed her life vest and placed it beside her on the bench. "Well, how about the Cancer Research Institute? They pretty much cover it all."

"Perfect." Staring onto the dock, Ivan squinted, then frowned. "Is he waiting for you or me?"

Mary glanced up, saw what Ivan was seeing and felt her pulse jump inside her veins. Standing there, arms crossed and looking murderous, was Ethan. "That would be for me."

Six

Ethan's body tightened at the sight of Mary walking down the dock toward him. A white T-shirt, pink shorts and bare feet had never looked so dangerous on any woman. Visions swam in his mind, images of soft skin against his mouth and long legs wrapped around his waist, cute round buttocks cupped in his hands. This intense physical reaction was becoming way too familiar, and he wondered if the only way he was going to get rid of it was to take her to bed again.

Ethan had known many women in his time, but his need for them had faded quickly. Why wasn't it the same with Mary Kelley? Why had the desire to taste her, fill his nostrils with her scent, open her thighs and bury himself deep inside her only intensified over time? Was it the baby or something else, something more?

Her pale-blue eyes mocked him as she came to stand before him, a grin tugging at her mouth. "You are officially stalking me now, Curtis."

"Well, one of us has to protect the baby," he muttered grimly.

"What in the world are you talking about?"

He gestured to the water. "Out there on the open water, no life jacket, no nothing."

"Open water?" she repeated, laughing. "Come on. This is a lake, calm as a sleeping kitten. There's no danger here."

Ethan eyed the man coming up behind her. "Isn't there?"

"Oh, for God's sake," Mary said as her sailboat buddy walked by with a smile and a wave. She waved back and called, "I'll call you on Thursday," then returned her attention to a very annoyed Ethan. "I was wearing a life jacket, and the captain—he's just a client."

"*The captain*," Ethan drawled with derision. "Please don't tell me that he makes you call him that?"

Mary regarded him incredulously. "Let's not get into crazy demands from clients, shall we?"

"Fine," he muttered darkly, following her down the dock and toward the parking lot.

As she dug the car keys from her purse, she asked, "Now, what's brought you all the way out here?"

"Do you have a doctor?"

She stopped, turned to look at him. "Why? Do you have a medical emergency?"

Her joke was lost on him and he scowled. "Be serious for a second."

"I have a doctor, Ethan."

"For the pregnancy?"

Her gaze flickered to the ground then back up, and he wondered if that was too intimate a thing to ask her.

"Yes, I have a doctor," she said finally. "A family-practice type thing. Why?"

He shook his head. "That's not good enough. You need an Ob/Gyn."

Exhaling heavily, she walked away from him toward the lot, but he was on her heels. "I'm serious, Mary."

"I'm going to come to your house and take every one of those books away from you. Foot massage is one thing, buddy, but—" she fumbled in her purse again for her keys "—you're getting way too knowledgeable on *Girlfriends' Guides* and *Mothering and You*, and frankly, it's making me feel a little weird."

Ethan paused. He didn't have those two books, but he made a mental note to get them. "Listen, I have a client whose wife is Deena Norrison."

"Never heard of her."

"She's only one of the best Ob/Gyn's in the country."

When Mary reached her car and still couldn't find her keys, she looked ready to explode. Undeterred, Ethan continued, "She's agreed to see you."

"I have a good doctor, Ethan," Mary assured him, her

hand stuffed inside her purse again, perspiration beading on her brow.

"Good is not great, and Deena's the best. Doesn't our child deserve the best?"

"Aha!" Mary held up her keys triumphantly, but her glee was short-lived when she noticed the stern look on Ethan's face. She sighed. "When is this appointment? This week is swamped for me, and next week we leave for Mackinac Island."

"How's today?"

"Today," she repeated, the blood draining from her face.

"Right now." He took her cool hand in his. "There's no reason to be nervous. I'm sure everything is fine."

"Now?"

"I know. Isn't that great? She's a pretty cool lady. She'll fit you in at four. Ultrasound and everything."

Mary shook her head. "But—"

Ethan didn't give her time to refuse. Once she saw the kid's heartbeat and heard from the best doctor in the country that everything was just as it should be, she'd relax. "Come on," he said, gently guiding her toward his car. "I'll drive."

Dr. Deena Norrison's reception area looked like a photograph straight out of the pages of *Victoria* magazine. Surrounded by cabbage-rose wallpaper, clients sank down into soft and cushy deep-pink sofas with rolled arms. The love seats and chairs, Mary was certain, had down pillows.

Mary sat on one of the love seats, her purse perched on the Queen Anne table before her. The scent of flowers was dizzying and made her feel as though she was trapped inside an English garden at the height of summer.

"Are you okay?" Ethan asked beside her.

"No. I don't know." The deodorant she'd put on this morning had disappeared, and she felt wet and uncomfortable.

"I can get you some water or something?" Ethan suggested.

The woman at the front desk stood, smiled at them and said in a polite whisper, "Mrs. Curtis?"

"Oh, jeez," Mary muttered.

"We can correct that later," Ethan assured her, then turned to the receptionist and said, "She's right here."

"We'll be taking you back soon," the woman informed them.

Mary saw it all in her mind: an examination table covered in a crisp old English linen sheet with exquisite crocheted trim and white slip-covered booties on the stirrups. She giggled a little hysterically.

"You need to relax," Ethan suggested gently.

"Easy for you to say," Mary uttered as the receptionist held out a clipboard with a flower pen attached.

"If you can just fill out this paperwork."

Sensing that Mary was not about to move, Ethan retrieved the papers for her and placed them in her lap. "I could do this if—"

"No, it's fine."

As Mary filled out the forms, the words blurred

together, and she had to stop and take a deep breath. The front door to the office opened and a woman came in. She was really far along in her pregnancy and looked exhausted. She dropped down in the chair beside Mary's love seat and exhaled heavily. When she spotted Mary, she smiled. "Long way to go yet, huh? When are you due?"

"What? Oh…ah…" It was all she could get out. Her heart pounded furiously in her chest, and waves of nausea were hitting her every few minutes. She needed air, needed to breathe something other than that damn flower smell. Suddenly panicked, she stood, dropped the paperwork on the table and ran out of the office. She spotted a stairwell to her left and ran to the door. Down the stairs she flew, her shirt spotted with sweat, her breathing labored. She heard Ethan behind her, calling her name, but she didn't stop. Once she made it to the lobby, she swung the front door open wide and ran to a grassy spot where a few nurses were eating their lunch.

Breathing heavily, she wanted to collapse on the grass, but instead she started pacing.

"Mary?"

She didn't look at him, didn't stop moving. "I can't do this."

"It's okay." His voice was soothing, and she hated him for his concern. He was the one who'd gotten them into this mess in the first place, damn him. "You don't have to see her," he continued. "Use your own doctor. I just thought it would be—"

"It's not the doctor, Ethan."

"Then what?" When she wouldn't stop pacing, he grabbed her shoulders and held her against him, his tone worried now. "What the hell is wrong?"

His chest felt so strong and she wanted to sink into it, disappear inside of it, but he wouldn't allow her to hide. Easing one hand from her shoulder, he tipped her chin up so she had to look at him.

"Tell me what's going on, Mary."

Miserably, she shook her head. "There is no baby."

"What?"

"No baby, Ethan."

He went white. "Did something happen…that boat ride…"

"No." She stared at him, into those beautiful dark-blue eyes she'd believed for so long were soulless. What a damn mess. This whole thing. "I just wanted my father to be okay."

He still looked confused, but after a moment, re-alization dawned and confusion was swapped for a fiercely accusing gaze. "You were never pregnant?"

Shame coiled in her belly and she shook her head. "No."

"You were never pregnant," he repeated.

"I'm sorry."

Ethan stared at her, his eyes wide in fury. "Yes, you will be," he uttered, his jaw knotted with the force of emotion.

"Ethan."

"I should've known."

"Ethan, please, I—" But her words fell on deaf ears. He had already turned his back on her and was stalking toward his car. Feeling as though she'd just assaulted someone, Mary dropped onto a hard picnic bench and watched his BMW leave the parking lot, tires squealing.

Seven

Twenty minutes later, Ethan entered the crumbling stone gates of Days of Grace Trailer Park. As he drove past the shabby office, muscle memory took hold and his BMW practically steered itself to the curb beside number fifty-three. The one-bedroom mobile home his father had sold just before his death looked as though it had been remodeled, as though someone were really trying to make the place a home, with fresh paint, a nice carport and fenced garden.

"About damn time," Ethan muttered, opening his window a crack before killing the engine.

It was ironic. At sixteen, he couldn't have gotten out of this park fast enough. He'd had big dreams, big plans, and he'd sworn to himself he'd never be back. But here he was, drawn to it like scum to bathroom tile. How was it that he felt infinitely more comfortable parked outside his father's trailer than at his home or office? Why was it that he could breathe here? The air was stale and slightly mildewed; nothing had changed.

He shoved a hand through his hair. He should have expected Mary to lie to him. People were never honest, never to be trusted—including himself. Why the hell hadn't he learned that in all this time? Maybe because he'd thought himself worthy of a family, good enough to make a child with a Harrington.

A large man in his early thirties wearing a baseball hat and ripped jeans came out of the house. When he spotted Ethan, he lifted a hand in a wary hello. Wasn't the first time the guy had seen Ethan parked there, but he'd never called security. No doubt the guy knew he could've handled the situation himself if things got out of control. After all, he was pretty big.

Not looking for any more trouble today, Ethan gunned the engine of his sports car and took off back to his self-made world.

Mondays were usually Mary's best day. She was well rested, coffeed-up and excited to get back to work. Today, however, she felt as though a semi had been driving back and forth over her body all night long. She felt jittery and exhausted at the same time—a wicked combination.

As she walked into the office, her hand shook a little around the double espresso she carried. The first person she saw was Olivia. The startlingly pretty brunette was sitting at the receptionist's desk—something she liked to do before Meg, the receptionist, got there at nine. "Hey there, Miss Kelley," she said in a chipper voice. "You're here early."

"And I'm not the only one."

"I have some phone calls to return. I wanted to get to them early." Olivia's eyes narrowed as she stared hard at Mary. "Did you get any sleep last night?"

Mary sighed, placed her plastic coffee cup on the reception desk. "I think somewhere between four and six I dozed off."

"Work…or—" Olivia hesitated, bit her full bottom lip "—something else?"

For a moment Mary contemplated blowing Olivia's mind with the entire story of Ethan Curtis and her. She just wanted to unburden herself with a girlfriend for a few minutes, emotionally puke and have Olivia figuratively hold her hair back. But for good or bad, the partners of NRR just didn't go there with each other— though Mary wondered if any of them wanted to but were afraid to ruffle the feathers of their business.

"I was working late," Mary said at last. "The captain is very demanding."

Olivia laughed at that, her dark eyes filled with mirth. "He seems like a semidecent guy, despite the millions and the bawdy reputation."

"He is, actually. Did I tell you he's donating all the proceeds from the regatta gala to charity?"

"Would it be uncharitable of me to say that he should?"

It was Mary's turn to laugh, though the sound felt a little forced. "Ivan's all right. Not much going on upstairs, though."

"What a shocker," Olivia said sarcastically. "Inherited wealth?"

"Yes."

Olivia rolled her eyes as she stood up and headed into the kitchen. "Do you want something to eat? I made blueberry muffins, and, not to toot my own horn or anything, but both attorneys offices downstairs came up to ask where that amazing scent was coming from."

Mary's stomach rolled rudely at the thought of food and she headed toward her office. "Maybe later."

"Okay. Oh, hey, Mary?"

"Yeah."

"Mr. Curtis called."

Mary felt a tremor of nervous energy move through her, and suddenly she felt unable to breathe. She hadn't spoken to him since Saturday, since her breakdown in the parking lot.

She poked her head out of her office and gave Olivia a weak smile. "Let me guess. He no longer requires my services."

Wielding a saucepan in one hand and an egg in the other, Olivia looked perplexed. "No. Actually, he asked if you could come by his house today at four-thirty."

"What?" There was no way she had heard Olivia correctly.

"Four-thirty," Olivia repeated. "His house."

"Oh. Okay." Well, sure. Why should he make the

trip to her office to can her when he could do it in person? Her heart pounded so hard in her chest the movement actually hurt.

"Is he an inheritance jerk, too, Mary?"

Mary shook her head. "No, self-made all the way."

Olivia nodded. "I thought so. He always sounds down-to-earth when he calls. That's pretty refreshing."

Mary went back into her office on unsteady legs and dropped into the chair behind her desk. She had to be ready to hear whatever he had to say. There was no doubt he was going to fire her, but what if he wanted to tell her that he was bringing her father back up on charges?

The queasy, dizzy, anxiety-ridden feeling she'd been having since yesterday came back full force, and she put her head down on her desk. Her eyes remained open, and even in the semidarkness of her self-made tent, Mary saw what she'd collapsed upon. The plans for Ethan's nursery—a nursery she hadn't even begun. With a groan she pushed the plans off her desk and into the trash can.

Ethan's housekeeper, Sybil, who Mary had only seen twice before—right before the staff and caterers arrived for a party—answered the door with a vexed expression. "Hello, Ms. Kelley."

"How are you, Sybil?"

The woman released a weighty breath. "Mr. Curtis is in the game room. Let me show you the way."

"Game room?" Mary repeated, following behind the housekeeper. She'd been in Ethan's house several times and she'd never seen a game room.

Glancing over her shoulder, Sybil rolled her eyes. "It's where he goes when he's brooding."

Brooding? Mary tried not to register the shock she felt. First of all, she couldn't imagine Ethan showing anyone his emotions—it just wasn't his style. And second of all, did he know that the woman he paid to run his household talked about him this way? She'd bet not.

They passed the dining room and library, then rounded a curve into a hallway that Mary had never ventured down, or even remembered seeing. When they came to a door, Sybil knocked once, then said to Mary, "Here we are."

"Should I just go in?" Mary asked when she heard no answer.

Sybil nodded. "He's expecting you."

After the woman walked away, Mary gripped the knob and pushed the door open. For a good thirty seconds after entering the large room, Mary thought she'd just stepped into kid's fantasyland, Chucky Cheese. But since she didn't smell pizza or see a large, furry gray animal with whiskers, she knew she must be in Ethan's game room.

The room was a perfect square, with one wall devoted to windows that faced the backyard and lake. It was as if the room was meant to have a screen or drape down the center as a divider, as the right side was completely devoted to every arcade game imaginable. Being a fan of arcades from way back, Mary recognized skeet ball right away and smiled wistfully. There was also basketball, air hockey, pound the squirrel, racecar games and many more she saw but wasn't familiar with. Then there was the left side of the room, which couldn't have been more different. It was an office, with a very modern desk and furnishings in charcoal gray and chrome, and in the middle of it sat Ethan, reading the newspaper.

She had an urge to turn around and leave before he saw her, but instead she walked into the room and parked herself beside the foosball table. "Quite a setup you got here."

Still hidden behind the *New York Times*, Ethan muttered a terse, "These are all the things I couldn't afford when I was a kid. I wanted to have them now."

Mary Kelley was no genius, but she sure understood his meaning: he'd had nothing growing up and was hoping to give this to his child. The child he'd thought was coming. The child he'd blackmailed a woman into creating with him.

She got it, and she felt Sybil's pain, and she, too, rolled her eyes. Why couldn't he have been in his library beside the bar drinking like any normal pissed-off male?

She fiddled with the handles on the foosball table. "Do you play?"

"I rarely play games," he said, still masked by the *Times*.

Neither did she, and she was having quite enough of this one. "Listen, you wanted to see me."

"Yeah." The paper came down with a snap, and Mary saw his face for the first time since they'd stood outside the doctor's office and she'd told him the truth. As he stood and walked over to her, he looked like a determined, really angry devil, his black hair slightly spiky and his blue eyes fierce with a need to hurt. He stood close, stared into her eyes and said in a punishing voice, "I have never felt such disgust with anyone in my life."

It was a strange thing—in that moment, spurred on by those words, Mary's nerves suddenly lifted and she was no longer afraid of what he was going to do about her and her father. The only thing she felt in the moment was the need to strike back. "I know that feeling. I had it about a month ago. But we were standing in your office, not your playroom."

His eyes blazed. "What you did was beyond low."

"You're right."

"And you have nothing to say."

"Just this. Need I remind you that you basically forced me into—"

"I never forced you to do anything," he interrupted darkly. "It was your choice—"

"Choice?" she repeated. Was he kidding? "What choice did I have? Tell me that?"

"You could have walked away."

"And left my dad to…what? Go to jail. Never." She glared at him. "But you don't understand that kind of devotion, do you? You've never loved anyone that much— so damn much that you'd make a great sacrifice for them."

His gaze slipped to her belly.

She shook her head, not about to pity him. "No, Mr. Curtis. That wasn't a sacrifice. That was a *need* to be met, a blue-blooded medal to hang around your neck to make you finally feel worthy." His nostrils flared, and he looked dangerously close to exploding, but Mary wouldn't back down. "At least the child would've belonged to the old-money club, right? And maybe you, too, by association? No, it doesn't work that way." She was yelling now, frustrated at him, at herself. "They don't care about association, they only care about blood. Can you get that through your thick skull?"

When she stopped ranting, they both stood there, face-to-face, breathing heavily. His eyes had lost some of their heat and she wondered if she'd finally gotten through to him. But he didn't answer her, not that she expected him to. He had too much pride. Instead, he did as all highly successful business persons do—he went for the jugular.

"You're wondering if I'm going to file charges against your father now, aren't you?" he said evenly, his tone cool.

Mary wasn't about to deny it. "Of course."

"I'm not."

Shock slammed into her and she actually stuttered. "Wh-why?"

With a casual shrug, he left her and wandered over to the air hockey table where he picked up a paddle and examined it. "I've decided to close that chapter."

Mary couldn't contain her relief. Her father didn't have to worry about court or jail ever again. She wasn't about to thank Ethan, but she could feel the tension drain from her body and she sagged against the foosball table.

"But I do want something from you."

Ethan's words sent a shock of alarm through her tired limbs. "What?"

"Mackinac Island."

Oh, no. The trip to the beautiful Michigan island. She was supposed to have planned a party there, served as hostess, but how could that ever happen now? "You want me to recommend someone to take my place, right?" she asked hopefully.

"No."

"You can't be seriously considering—"

He slammed the paddle down and glared at her. "Believe me when I say I would rather bring a python with me on this trip. But your reputation has preceeded you, and I need that party to go off without a problem."

No way. She couldn't. There was too much between them. She shook her head. "No."

"You owe me."

"I owe you nothing," she assured him, straightening up, forcing her legs to hold her weight and not buckle.

His voice dropped and his lips thinned dangerously. "Don't think I wouldn't reconsider opening that paternal book again if I have to."

She shook her head, knowing she was cornered. "You're really good at blackmail."

He lifted one sardonic eyebrow. "I'll protect my business any way I have to."

"Clearly."

"Just as you would, Mary. Mine is administrative business and yours would be personal business."

The idea that they were in any way alike made Mary's blood jump in her veins, but she knew when her choices were few. "This will be our final business endeavor together."

He nodded. "After the last guest has left my party, Ms. Kelley, you and I can pretend that we've never met each other. How's that?"

"Perfect."

Eight

The airport was packed, but Mary maneuvered her way through the crowds with the fierce determination of a woman going to war. According to the itinerary Ethan's secretary had sent over yesterday morning, the plan was to fly to Chicago, then to Pellston Airport in Michigan, then take a cab to the Mackinac Island ferry. After their declarations of mutual disgust for each other, Mary was more than a little shocked that she and Ethan would be traveling together. She could've easily caught her own flight and met him at the hotel, but he'd insisted they make the trip together.

After checking in and making it through security without a body search, Mary headed over to the gate to wait for Ethan. She winced as she slid her carry-on bag off her shoulder and onto one of the hard plastic chairs.

The captain's regatta gala had been successful yesterday, raising a huge amount of money for the Cancer Research Institute, but Mary had forgotten to apply a liberal coat of sunscreen and had managed to give herself quite a sunburn in the process. And the painful moments just kept coming as she spotted Ethan walking toward her, looking anything but the stuffy business traveler in a long-sleeved white shirt and jeans, his large frame and hawklike gaze sending people out of his way without a word from him.

"Ms. Kelley."

Her body instantly betrayed her, her insides jumping with awareness at the sound of his voice. "Mr. Curtis."

"You look well," he said, barely glancing at her striped polo shirt and white cropped jeans.

"Ah…thanks," she muttered with a touch of sarcasm.

Ignoring her tone, Ethan handed her a large envelope. "I've taken the liberty of providing a dossier on the potential clients we're going to see. Their likes, dislikes, food preferences and hobbies."

"Great." Mary couldn't help but notice all the wistful stares Ethan was getting from women walking past. No wonder he could be so arrogant.

"As far as staff to hire for the party goes," he continued brusquely, "I have the name of the best—"

"I've already been in touch with several staff-for-hire agencies on the island," Mary informed him proudly. "I know who I'm going to hire and have already spoken to most of the staff."

The only sign that Ethan might be impressed by her actions was the slight lift of his brows. "You're nothing if not on top of matters, are you?"

Mary couldn't tell if his words were meant as a back-handed compliment or sexual innuendo, but she flashed him a defiant glance regardless. "I'm good at what I do, how about that?"

"Make-believe," he muttered.

"Excuse me?"

"A wife-for-hire agency, Mary?" he stated, as if that said it all. "What is that but pretending to be someone else?"

Mary was silent for a moment, her ire moderated by observation. "You know, I think there's hope for you yet, Curtis."

"I guess it's my turn to say, excuse me?"

"If you can recognize the phony in me, you'll be able to see it in yourself soon enough."

Before Ethan could even react to her words, a woman approached them with a plastered-on smile. "Mr. Curtis, you may board now if you wish. The first-class cabin is ready."

"Thank you."

Ready to follow him, Mary shouldered her bag. "Should I go with you or are we boarding separately?"

A slow grin touched Ethan's mouth, and he nodded at her boarding pass. "Better check your seat assignment first."

Confused, Mary looked down at the ticket in her hand. When she looked back up, Ethan was already on his way toward the gate. How lovely, she mused. While he got pampered with warm towels and chocolate chip cookies in first class, she was going to share a bathroom with forty other passengers in coach.

"What's wrong with your neck?" Ethan asked her once they were aboard the ferry and headed for Mackinac Island.

"It's nothing," she grumbled.

"Nothing my ass," he countered as they walked the length of the deck and back again. "You're moving like a robot."

Ethan was just full of compliments, and she felt like socking him. "It's just a pulled muscle. No big deal."

"You can't meet clients like that."

"It'll pass, okay? Relax."

"How did it happen?"

The wind off the water whipped Mary's hair around her neck as she tried to pick up her pace and shake off the stiffness in her limbs. "Do you really care? Why don't you go inside and have a cup of coffee or a bourbon or something and let me work out these kinks myself."

"I care, okay?" he said dryly. "What the hell happened on the flight?"

She sighed, stopped in her tracks and faced him. "A very large man decided to take a nap on my shoulder, and no amount of pushing and prodding and poking would wake him up. I was stuck in this insanely awkward position for two hours. I wonder if they have a chiropractor on the island."

Ethan stared at her.

"What?" she asked.

"You poked someone?"

She sighed with heavy patience. "It was just with the eraser end of a pencil." But, oh, how she had wanted to do so much more. "Little good it did. It only made him snore harder. And don't even get me started with the lady on my right."

"Did you poke her, too?"

"No, but I thought about it." Mary pressed a hand to her lower back and stretched out her spine a little.

"Wanted to tell you her life story?"

"No. But that would've been okay, life story I could've handled. I can work up a good conversation with a stranger." Her memory of the woman was pretty fresh and a wave of nausea hit her full-on. "No, this was a lack-of-deodorant thing."

Amusement played behind his eyes. "I'm not going to feel sorry for you."

"Who asked you to?" she returned playfully, using every ounce of will to make herself start walking again.

"You belonged in coach."

She gave him a mock bow. "I know that, Mr. Curtis. I'm an employee, and I'm cool with that. In work and in life I know who I am and where I belong, and I fully accept it." She couldn't help herself, the words just fell out. "Unlike other people."

"What's that supposed to mean?" he asked as they reached the railing.

Only wanting to make a quick dig, not have a full-on fight, Mary glanced over the edge to the choppy sea below and tried to deflect. "Look at that water."

Ethan wasn't having any of it. Not that she expected him to. "Don't go all female on me, Mary."

Mary considered. "I don't think that was as much female as it was passive-aggressive."

"Whatever it was, just say what you've got to say," he said impatiently.

She exhaled and turned to face him. "This is just a thought, but maybe if you'd stop trying to be something you're not, you could actually enjoy your success. Maybe you wouldn't have to resort to blackmailing people into doing what you want. They might come willingly."

He grinned then, his gaze moving lazily over her. "If I remember correctly you came very willingly."

"Don't be crude."

He shrugged, looking like a bad little boy. "I was talking about coming to work for me. But I like where your dirty mind goes, Ms. Kelley."

"If you remember correctly, working for you was something I fought tooth and nail."

"I remember you giving in pretty quickly, actually, as though you wanted to be as close to me as I wanted to be to you."

Were they always going to end up here? Mary wondered. Bantering back and forth, both wanting to outsmart and outplay the other. And to what end...? It was only a few more days. "All I'm saying is that if you'd accept who you are and where you came from maybe you could be happy."

"Who says I want to be happy?"

"Everyone's looking for happiness, in some form or another."

"Not me."

She ignored him. "The problem is you're going about it the wrong way."

He gave his back to the water and lounged against the railing. "And you know the way to true happiness, Mary?"

No, but... "I'm trying. I'm sure as hell trying." She cocked her head to the left to look at the island as it came into view and felt a searing pain in her neck. She groaned.

Ethan cursed softly. "You can hardly turn your head."

"I'm fine. Nothing that a hot shower and a massage won't cure."

He touched her shoulder. "You know, I'd offer to help you with both of those forms of physical therapy, but—"

"But you pretty much hate me right now," she answered, trying to ignore the heat from his hand.

"Nope, that logic doesn't matter so much for a guy."

She tried to look shocked, but laughter quickly bubbled in her throat. "Okay, so what is it, then? You can't help me take a shower because *I* can't stand *you*?"

He considered this for about two seconds. "Ah...no. A guy can get past that sad fact, too."

She laughed again.

His voice lowered to a sexy timbre. "And you don't hate me, Mary."

His arrogance and unflinching confidence could be a real pain in the ass sometimes, especially when his assumptions were right on target. "Well, so what is it, then? Don't tell me you won't assist my shower time out of some misplaced sense of duty."

"No." He faced the coming island and looked pensive. "I'm just afraid it might make me happy, and as I said, I'm not looking for that."

The Birches was an authentic 1890s Queen Anne Victorian, and when Mary first stepped inside the entryway, she thought she'd fallen asleep and woken up in a dream—or at the very least a movie. The nine-bedroom, six-bath original Victorian had beautifully restored hardwood floors, luscious paneled ceilings, three fireplaces, extensive property, and from the wraparound porch, a panoramic view of the Straits of Mackinac, Round Island, Mackinac Bridge and the Grand Hotel.

She couldn't even imagine how much it cost to rent such a place. Harold, the real estate agent Ethan had used for their trip, gestured gleefully around himself. "Here we are, Mr. Curtis. Beautiful home, isn't it."

"Nice," Ethan said unenthusiastically as he checked his Blackberry.

Poor Harold looked so dejected that Mary felt compelled to offer up her best smile. "Well, I think it's lovely."

He gave her a grateful look. "It was rumored that Rudolph Valentino and Nita Naldi stayed here at one time."

"Really?"

"Right after *Blood and Sand*."

"Wasn't Valentino married?"

Harold nodded and said conspiratorially, "To two women, actually. He hadn't yet divorced the other."

"I hate silent films," Ethan muttered, checking his e-mail.

Mary rolled her eyes at Harold. "So, where am I staying?"

Before Harold could even open his mouth, Ethan jumped in with, "I arranged for you to have the house next door."

"What?" Mary looked from Ethan to Harold and back again. "A whole house? Come on, Curtis. I thought I'd just get a hotel room close by."

Harold cleared his throat, his neck growing as red as a ripe tomato as he tried to make eye contact with Ethan. "Actually, sir, we had an emergency, and the family staying there had to remain on. But," he said, brightening, "we have a lovely suite for Ms. Kelley across town at the Mackinac Inn."

"That will be fine," Mary said pleasantly, but she could feel Ethan already shaking his head.

"No, it won't," he informed her. "We have work to do, and you need to be here. Across town…" he said in a tone that sounded as though she were going to stay somewhere in Paris. "You can't even get anywhere around here without a horse or a bicycle. It'll take forever."

"Sir," Harold attempted deferentially. "I assure you that on an island so small, transportation is quick and very easy to—"

Ethan ignored him, his gaze hard and fixated on Mary. "You'll stay with me."

She was getting awfully tired of Ethan Curtis's demands. "No way."

"This house is large enough for ten people," he said.

"Again. No way."

He scowled. "You're acting like a child."

"I'm acting like a professional. Forget for a moment how it looks and feels to me, but how would it look to your clients if the woman you hired is also staying in the home you rented?"

He shrugged. "Practical."

"No." She lowered her voice as Harold pretended to inspect a wall sconce. "Like she's also being hired for another purpose."

They stared at each other, a haze of lust blanketing Ethan's expression. Mary felt helpless, weak for a moment as a quick shiver shot through her. She tried to control the sudden pounding of her heart, until finally the look on Ethan's face dissolved.

"You're being paranoid," he said roughly. "This is business. I'll have offices here and so will you. You can take the entire second floor and I'll remain down here. Barring business, we never have to see each other."

Mary sighed. She didn't want to argue the point anymore, and poor, miserable Harold had all but tried to crawl up inside the wall sconce and disappear. She would figure out her situation on her own. "All right, Harold. Can you show me upstairs?"

The man released a weary breath and started up the

stairs. "There are some beautiful rooms to choose from and incredible views of the water."

Before she followed him, Ethan put his hand on her shoulder. "Make sure you get that shower. You're still walking like a robot." Then he leaned in, whispered in her ear, "And if you need any help…"

Yes, she'd have to find another arrangement as soon as possible. Just the warmth of Ethan's hand made her want to curl into him, nuzzle his neck and remove his shirt, but she detached herself anyway, and followed the agent up the stairs. "Hey, Harold, how old is this house did you say?"

"It was built in 1891, but everything's been updated for your convenience."

"Like the plumbing?"

"Of course."

"And locks on the doors?"

"Every one of them, miss."

She heard Ethan chuckle below, and the sound shot to every nerve, every muscle, every spot that ached for his touch.

Nine

Good thing he'd checked the house's extensive property, or he might not have found her.

The historic barn was only about sixty feet from the main house and featured three horse stalls, food storage areas, tack room, carriage storage room, hay room and small living quarters upstairs. That last bit of information had tipped Ethan off when Mary hadn't come downstairs after a shower and change.

Ethan scowled at her. "You're the most stubborn person I have ever met."

Wearing a white terry cloth robe that showed absolutely nothing except for her feet and about an inch of neck, Mary stood at the barn door, blocking his entrance. "Thank you."

"That agent told you about this place, didn't he?"

"His name is Harold."

"Yeah, well, Harold clearly isn't looking for a good word from me to his boss."

"Don't take it out on Harold," Mary said, trying to force her hair into some type of halo style on top of her head with a couple of pins. She looked like a damn angel and Ethan had an intense urge to be saved.

"Are you going to show me around?" Ethan asked wryly.

Defiance glimmered in her pale-blue eyes, but she took a step back and allowed him to pass. "Do you promise to be good?"

"Are you kidding? Don't you know me at all?"

She laughed, a soft, throaty sound that made him think of the nights they'd shared, the sound that would erupt from her throat every time she climaxed. Blood thrummed in his temples as he followed her past the neat tack room and unused stalls, up the short set of stairs to the loft. There he took one look around and sniffed derisively. "This place is microscopic and—"

"And perfect for one person," Mary finished for him.

The walk upstairs had caused the ties on her robe to loosen, and the lapels were gaping slightly—just enough for him to see a curve of one pale breast. His mouth watered, and he tore his gaze away and glared at the bed. Warm light infused the room, kissing the pale-blue coverlet. It was a soft space, and he felt way too hard to belong there.

"I think it's the best of both worlds," Mary said, mistaking his tense jaw and piercing gaze for annoyance instead of desire. "Seeing how we feel about each other."

How they felt about each other. The idea made Ethan want to laugh. One minute he wanted to shake her, and the next he wanted to kiss her. What he did know was that he didn't want to hate her—not anymore—didn't want to feel pissed off at her. "I don't like this."

She sighed. "We're close enough to work and far enough not to…"

"Not to what?" he asked, wondering how long it would take him to remove that robe. Two seconds? Five? Or maybe he'd want to do it slowly, just a shoulder first. Or maybe he's start at her feet, work his way up to her calves, thighs… "Fall into bed again?"

Pink suddenly stained her cheeks, and she moistened her bottom lip with her tongue. "Something like that."

"It seems like a whole lot of trouble for nothing."

Her chin lifted. "I seem to remember you comparing me to a python. Aren't you glad that the python isn't living upstairs?"

He didn't answer. He walked over to the window and stared out. "There's no view of the water from here."

She sniffed. "I think I'll live."

"You'll be up here day and night…alone."

"Why do you care, Curtis?"

"I don't," he said through gritted teeth. He didn't want to.

"Business won't suffer," she assured him. "I can be up at the house in under five minutes."

If he didn't get the hell out of here right now, he was

going to find out the answer to that robe question of his, and then Mary Kelley would have the upper hand on him and he couldn't have that. He turned away from the window and stalked across the tiny space. "Thirty will be fine."

She studied him, her brows slightly knitted. "What's the plan for the rest of the day?"

"We have a few hours of good light left. Maybe… scouting a location for the party?"

She looked surprised. "I would've thought you'd want it at the house."

"I'm not sure what I want," he said tightly. "I'd like some options."

Her expression now impenetrable, she nodded. "All right. Well, I'm finally going to take that shower I've been looking forward to since this morning, and I'll meet you out front in thirty minutes."

The thought of Mary naked under a waterfall of hot water had Ethan sucking in oxygen, but not enough: his lungs constricted with pain. *She* was going to take off that robe, not him. *She* was going to touch her skin, not him. Women could be masters at torture, but this woman had it down to a science. His gaze shot to the small bathroom to his right. So white and clean and sweet.

His entire body charged with electricity, Ethan turned away and headed back down the stairs.

"We could always walk into town," Mary suggested as she sat in the back of a small black buggy, outside the gates of their rental house.

Glaring at the docile horse, Ethan slowly shook his head. "Nope."

The carriage driver looked straight ahead, smart enough not to get involved, but Mary wasn't afraid to incur the wrath of Ethan Curtis. The late-afternoon sun was starting to mellow into a stunning orangish pink and if they didn't get a move on they'd be scouting locations for the party in the dark.

"Are you going to climb up here or not?" Mary asked as she watched Ethan sidle up to the chestnut mare.

"Just give me a minute," he uttered crossly, reaching out to stroke the animal's mane as he whispered something to her Mary couldn't hear.

When he finally climbed into the buggy and dropped down beside Mary, she was curious as hell. "So, what's up with you and Shirley?"

"It was personal."

The driver clicked his tongue a few times and they were off down the dirt road. "Did you ask for her hand in marriage?" Mary asked, grinning. "Oops, sorry, I mean her hoof?"

"We were just having a little discussion, that's all."

"About?"

"Manners."

Mary laughed. "Did you have a drink before we left the house?"

Ethan crossed his arms over his chest and reclined back in his seat. "I don't want her throwing us, that's all."

"The driver said she's as docile as they come."

"That's what they'd like you to believe," he muttered dryly.

"They?"

"The driver and…Shirley."

Again she laughed. "What in the world are you talking about?"

"I'm not all that into horses, okay?"

"Oh, c'mon. Everyone loves horses. How could you not like horses? It's un-American."

"Okay, they don't like me," he grumbled.

"You need therapy," she said as they passed another horse and buggy on their way to town. The air had chilled considerably since their arrival, and Mary scooted just a little closer to Ethan. "All right, I'm listening. Tell me the whole sad story."

"What story?"

"Give me a break." She inched even closer to him so their legs were touching. "You've got to be freaked out for a reason—what's the story?"

On a curse, Ethan lifted his arm, dropped it around her shoulders. "I was ten. It was Sammy Bishop's birthday party and this sweet and supposedly ancient horse named Izabo was there giving rides to all the kids. With everyone else, she walked slower than a turtle, it was almost funny, the parents were actually referring to her IzaSlow. But as soon as *I* got on her back it was Kentucky Derby time." He lifted up his left forearm. "I fell and broke my arm in three places."

Mary let her head relax against his arm, knowing full well how totally inappropriate they were both being.

"That was a fluke thing and it happened one time. You can't hold that against—"

"Then when I was fourteen," he said as the buggy took a deep hole and they bumped against each other. "My girlfriend dragged me to the circus. Everything was fine until the horse and rider came out. Jezebel the Great freaked out halfway through her routine and stormed the stands."

"No way."

"Oh, yeah. And who do you think she headed straight for?"

"Okay, I'm beginning to see a pattern," Mary said, laughing, the scent of lake water heavy in the air.

"I broke two ribs."

Without thinking, Mary reached over and ran her fingers down the length of his rib cage only stopping when she heard his sharp intake of breath. "Feel fine to me."

His heavy-lidded gaze held hers. "Well sure, they've healed now."

It was a good thing that the driver stopped then, or Mary believed Ethan might've leaned in and kissed her, and she also believed she would have kissed him back. They got out in front of a fudge shop and started walking up Main Street, which had a similar architectural feel to New Orleans, though the scents in the air were totally different. As they passed shops, restaurants and art galleries, Mary missed Ethan's arm around her, the strength of him, and she silently wished he'd take her hand, lace her fingers with his.

"You know what?" she said as they walked to the

west end of downtown where the pedestrians were fewer. "I don't think it's really about the horses not liking you."

"Oh, this should be interesting."

"I think it's a sex thing."

A dark brow lifted over one eye. "Come again?"

"Izabo, Jezebel and Shirley," she pointed out. "It's a female thing. Females have this reaction to you."

Ethan processed this for a brief moment, then burst out laughing. "How the hell did I get mixed up with you?"

She tossed him a taunting smirk. "Do you really want me to answer that?"

They continued down the street, passing a lovely old church, a library and a quaint soda shop—which Mary considered for the party, then quickly deemed too informal. Several blocks down, closer to the water, Ethan pointed to a lovely, small, intimate hotel called the Miran Inn. "What do you think of this place?"

Cocking her head to one side, Mary looked the inn up and down. "It's beautiful, but hotels have been done to death. Not to mention the fact that three of the ten potential clients we're throwing this party for own inns on the island."

"Right."

"Don't you want something interesting and surprising? Something the spouses actually want to come to?"

"Yes."

Mary had been contemplating something since they'd arrived here, and she wanted to pull it out now. "Let's go." Grabbing his hand, she tugged, urging him to follow her.

"Where?"

"Just follow me."

Mary led him off the main street and down a short hill to a bluff, onto the sandy beach. Overhead the gulls were calling on each other to share their fish, and several tourists were taking pictures of a beautiful lighthouse in the distance. Releasing his hand, Mary walked down to the water's edge and lifted her hands to the fading sun. "Perfect," she called, turning back to face him. "A barbecue on the beach. Intimate, casual, great food— and no horses involved."

Ethan glanced around, then slowly nodded. "I like it."

"Great," she said excitedly. It would be her first beachside barbeque and she was going to make it a day to remember.

Ethan came to stand beside her, a look of admiration in his eyes. "I have to admit, you're great at what you do, you know that?"

Her hair whipped around her face. "Thank you."

He tucked one thick blond strand behind her ear, then let his thumb retreat across her cheek. "Very smart, very intuitive. There's just one problem."

Her expression froze. "What's that?"

"You're too beautiful for your own good. A man couldn't get you out of his mind no matter how pissed off he was."

"Don't you mean 'is'?" He was too close. She could feel the heat off his body, and there was no denying the desire in his eyes.

His fingers left her cheek and slid down her neck,

pausing at her collarbone. He didn't move for a moment, and his face looked rigid, as if he was contemplating what he'd just done. Then he dropped his hand and shook his head helplessly. "I'm sorry. I...I have to get back."

Electricity was shooting through Mary's body like fireworks, but she fought for control and nodded once. "Of course."

"I have a dinner meeting."

"And I have a guest list to study."

They walked side by side, up the bluff and back to Main Street to catch a cab.

"You'll be all right on your own tonight?" Ethan asked as one pulled up in front of them.

Mary climbed into the cab and this time sat close to the door. "Have been for the past twenty-some years," she uttered softly.

"What was that?" Ethan asked, not having heard her muffled answer.

She released a heavy sigh. "I said, I'll be just fine."

At night on Mackinac Island something wonderful happens. As the sun sets slowly and exquisitely against the water, the sounds of nature hum rhythmically through an invisible speaker. Forget expensive sound machines to soothe you to sleep, opening a window and stretching out on the bed was all Mary needed for a relaxing evening.

Well, that and some food...and a glass of wine.

With several pillows behind her head, Mary grabbed the delivery menus she'd garnered from the buggy driver and flipped through them. Beside her on the table was the guest list she now knew backward and forward, and she was ready to chill out. She paused on the page of an Italian menu that sounded pretty good and grabbed her cell phone off the bedside table. But before she had completed dialing the number, there was a sharp rap on the door downstairs.

She glanced at the clock. Would Ethan really be done with his dinner meeting by eight-thirty? Maybe it was Harold, come to discuss the history of each barn stall and let her know that Man O' War once sired a foal here. Laughing at her idiocy, Mary loped down the stairs and hauled back the barn door.

Ethan Curtis leaned against the door frame looking incredibly handsome in jeans and a black long-sleeved T-shirt, his sharp jaw dusted with stubble.

"Everything okay?" Mary asked, amusement in her voice.

"Yeah," he began, then took it back. "Well, no. There's a problem up at the main house."

"Seriously? What is it? Did a pipe burst or something? These older houses are notorious for plumbing problems no matter how new the pipes…"

"No. It's not the pipes."

"Fireplace smoking?"

"No."

She just loved it when he was forthcoming. "Well, what is it? Can't figure out which bed to sleep in?"

His eyes darkened. "Something like that."

Instinctively she took a step back, but only managed

to knock her heel against a bucket and feel like a clumsy oaf. "How did your meeting go?"

"Good, fine, boring," he said, his gaze moving over her. "They're looking forward to the barbecue."

Mary nodded, her mouth suddenly numb. If he would only just grab her, make this easy on both of them.

"Oh…" Ethan pulled a plastic bag from behind his back and handed it to her. "I thought if you hadn't eaten…"

"Thanks. I was just about to order something."

"Now you don't have to."

Many different ways of asking, "Would you like to share this with me?" popped into Mary's head, but she rejected all of them. After all, he'd just come from dinner with clients. "Well, I'm going to go and enjoy this."

"Okay." He didn't move.

She raised a brow at him and tried to apply a professional tone. "Do we need to discuss anything or can it wait until morning?"

He walked past her into the barn, his hand brushing over hers as he took the takeout bag from her. "You know what? I don't think it can wait."

Ten

Ethan hadn't been kidding about the dinner he'd just had with two potential clients. The food had been ordinary, the conversation bland, and somewhere around the caprese salad, he'd hoped for a fire in the kitchen so an immediate evacuation would send him back to The Birches.

Mary followed him up the stairs to the loft, her tone warily playful. "Something tells me that inviting you in may turn out to be dangerous."

"Perceptive," he said over his shoulder.

"So if you come in, can we talk about the menu?"

"I'm already in, but sure." At the moment, Ethan could care less about the menu for the barbecue. He was in Mary's room, surrounded by moonlight and the subtle soapy scent of her. Hell, at this moment, he couldn't care less about work, clients or good manners.

Her back to the wall, Mary gestured around the room. "Not many places to sit."

Ethan glanced at the bed, then back at her. "No."

Looking suddenly self-conscious in her pink tank top and matching boy shorts, Mary eyed the bathroom door. "I should throw on a robe or something."

"Don't go to any trouble for me."

"I think I'm already in trouble," she muttered, walking over to the bedside table and grabbing a yellow legal pad. "So, the caterer thinks—and I agree with her—that an all-American barbecue would be best. Ribs, burgers, barbecued chicken, sweet-potato fries, salads, pecan and apple pies. And maybe some local flavors like fresh cherried whitefish."

Didn't she get it? Ethan wondered, dropping the takeout bag on the window seat. She could move across the room, across the yard or all the way across the island and it wouldn't make a damn bit of difference. He'd still come for her, he'd still seek her out—his need for her was that strong.

"Some of the local menu items are interesting," she continued, her breathing slightly labored as she spoke, as though she'd just ran the loft stairs. "We could have a tasting if you'd like."

"I'd like that."

His tone and meaning were clear as the night sky outside the window, and Mary shook her head, her pale-blue eyes uneasy. "We can't."

"We won't."

Mary's skin suddenly felt very tight, as if she'd spent weeks in the sun without protection, and she tossed him a look that said, "Yeah, right." They were leading up to something here, something inevitable, proven even further by the fact that Ethan was walking toward her right now.

"I swear I won't even go near the bed," he said. Ethan brought his hands up and cupped her face, the warmth of his skin melting all of her resolve in an instant. She leaned toward him as he dipped his head and covered her mouth in a series of soul-crashing kisses.

He was so warm as his mouth and his chest brushed teasingly against her breasts that Mary's knees nearly buckled, and she wrapped her arms around Ethan's neck for support. His body responding at once, Ethan groaned at the nearness and gently pressed her back against the wall, cradling her neck in his hand as he explored her mouth with teasing, drifting kisses until she opened for him, gave him a sweep of her tongue.

Mary tried to keep her head, tried to recall what they had said to each other just the other day, the rotten things they'd said, but each thought faded away like fog in the sun. She felt his hand delve under her shirt, felt his palm on her stomach and sucked air through her teeth, her back arching as she silently begged him to explore higher.

Pressing closer to her, Ethan reached around her with his free hand and unhooked her bra, setting her free while holding her captive with his mouth. Mary could hardly remain still. Her skin itched to be touched, and when his hand raked up her torso and covered one full breast, when he slowly rolled the hard peak between his thumb and forefinger, she cried out into his mouth.

The sound had Ethan backing off for a moment, his hungry gaze fixated on her. Thinking he was about to scoop her up and deposit her on the bed, Mary shook her head wearily. "You swore you wouldn't—"

"Go near the bed," he finished for her. "And I'm not."

"Then…what are you—"

She never finished the sentence as Ethan lifted her shirt over her head and artfully cast aside her lacy bra. She stared at him, at his face, marveled at the need there as the lower half of her contracted and hummed.

"I wasn't hungry until now," he mumbled, dipping his head and nuzzling up one pale slope until he found the sustenance he required. His tongue circled her taut nipple slowly, desperately slowly, and Mary could only arch her back again and again, thrusting herself in and out of his mouth until finally he took her between his lips and tongue and suckled deep and hard.

"Oh, Ethan," she whispered breathlessly, her knees weak and the small curve at the top of her inner thigh wet with desire.

Ethan drank from her, his tongue flicking the swollen bud back and forth until her hips began to move, to thrust forward and back looking for his hand, his mouth, something to ease the building tension within her—or maybe to build it even further. His mouth moved down, gently sinking his teeth into her belly and hip bones as his hands brought her shorts and underwear to her ankles, then off completely.

Mary felt a moment of embarrassment, being fully naked in front of him, standing there in slashes of moonlight, her breasts free, one nipple still wet from his mouth, and the lower half of her open and ready for whatever he was willing to give.

On his knees, Ethan spared her one wicked, hungry glance before taking what he wanted. "Open your legs," he said, his warm breath so close to her sensitive flesh that Mary found it almost impossible to hold on to the climax she felt building just inches from his mouth.

She widened her stance and let her eyelids drift closed, tried to calm her body, ease the electric charges running through at a sprint, but when he spread the soft folds back with his thumbs, she couldn't control anything anymore. When he lapped at her with his tongue, Mary groaned and pressed herself against him. When he suckled and nuzzled the tender bud beneath, she cried out his name, "Ethan, please, I can't…"

She had no idea what she couldn't do, if it was hold on to her climax or give in to him or both, her mind was adrift on a sea of all-consuming pleasure. Then his hands came around to her buttocks, squeezing the flesh as he found his rhythm, his tongue flicking the tiny nub over and over as Mary rocked her hips.

"I can't hold on…" she uttered, her limbs weak, her body charged with electricity as the waves crashed and she stiffened—every part of her but her hips. She cried out and rocked wildly against his mouth, shuddering, giving in to release.

Mary sagged against the wall, her hips still bucking,

but slowly now as she sucked air through her teeth and tried to force back rational thought to her mind. When Ethan left her to stand, she felt slightly cold, but he took her in his arms and held her against him, his heart thundering so powerfully she could feel it against her chest. More than anything, she wanted him to take her to the bed, rise up over her and sink down between her legs. For a moment she thought about pushing him back onto the bed and straddling him, taking what she wanted as he had just taken from her.

But she never got the chance. She was still shaking from head to toe when Ethan moved away from her. He walked into the bathroom and came back with her robe, which he gently placed around her. Then he found her gaze and uttered a gentle, "I'll go."

"You don't have to," she said boldly, not really giving a damn that she sounded needful and not the littlest bit desperate.

He ran a hand through his hair and looked uncomfortable, shaken…or was that angry? She couldn't tell. "I really do."

She quickly slipped her arms through the holes in the robe, then nodded at Ethan. What the hell else could she do? "So, tomorrow…"

"Ten. On the porch." It was all he said before heading down the stairs and out of the barn.

Mary went to the window, watched him walk across the yard, her knees still trembling with aftershocks of her climax, the relaxing sounds of nature now replaced by the hum in her body—the need for more. If she'd had her way—and Ethan could've handled it, if he had the same unrelenting desire that she felt for him—he'd be poised above her right now, spreading her legs again, but this time for an entirely different purpose.

The image caused such intense shots of electricity to run through her body that she had to sit down on the edge of the bed.

Mary left City Hall with permits for the party and walked through town, hoping to arrive back at Ethan's place just before their scheduled meeting time. She'd been up since five that morning, planning the party and keeping her mind focused on Ethan's business goals as well as her own—basically anything except what had happened last night. As she passed Ticklers Fudge Shoppe, her cell phone rang, making several passersby frown at the disturbance.

She flipped open the phone and pressed it to her ear. "Hello?"

"Hey, it's Tess," came the voice of her partner. "And Olivia," chirped the other. "We're conferencing you."

Mary had been on several trips, business and otherwise over the past five years and had rarely missed hearing from her partners. This morning, however, she felt incredibly comforted by the sound of their voices. "Hey, there. How are things back home?"

"Same old, same old," Olivia informed her. "And how is Mackinac Island? Insanely beautiful and romantic?"

"She's not there for romance, Olivia," Tess said, a bite of irritation in her tone.

"Of course she's not. I just meant—"

"It's lovely," Mary said with a laugh, passing the small church that was about three-quarters of a mile from The Birches, making her heart jump nervously at the thought of seeing Ethan in a few minutes. "Lovely and incredibly picturesque."

"Well, in that case," Tess began, her business tone smartly in place. "Make sure you take plenty of pictures for our book."

"I will," Mary promised. "So, besides checking on the beauty of the island, anything you two want to discuss—anything going on I should know about?"

"Well," Olivia said excitedly. "We wanted to tell you that we've gotten three calls from men who were at Mr. Curtis's party last week. Two older gentlemen whose wives have passed and who have no idea how to run a social or home life. By the way, they were very impressed with what you did and are desperate to hold similar events for their companies. One of them is selling his home and moving to a waterfront estate— he's terrified because his wife handled all of that type of detail."

"Sounds right up our alley," Mary said, very pleased that her efforts had brought NRR several more clients. "And what about the third?"

Olivia snorted. "One very arrogant thirty-something trust-fund baby."

"Oh, your favorite," Mary said, grinning.

"And Tess palmed him off on me," Olivia added sourly. Mary heard Tess groan in frustration, as though she'd had this conversation ten times already. "He needs your culinary skills."

The wind picked up around Mary, bringing the scent of overcast morning and lake water to her nostrils. "What's his name?"

"Mac Valentine," Olivia told her.

Mary racked her brain for a mental picture of him, then recalled the handsome man Ethan had introduced to her at the first party. Oh, yes. Everything Olivia despised. Family money, total playboy, gorgeous and knew it.

Olivia sighed. "It'll be fine. Just like the rest of you, I refuse to get sucked in by clients. Do my job and do it well, and that's it."

As she walked down the country lane, Mary spotted her "just a client" on the porch of the old Victorian home, mug in hand, and felt a shiver of awareness move through her. If the girls only knew what a mess she'd gotten herself into over this particular client, they'd probably kick her out of the business. "Got to go, ladies."

"Oh, one more thing," Tess said quickly. "Your grandmother has called here three times since you've been gone."

"Why didn't she try my cell?"

"She said she misplaced the number, so I gave it to her again. She sounded pretty agitated."

That's what came from not checking her messages at home or at the office. "She always sounds that way. Agitated is normal. Now if you said she sounded blissful or pleased, I'd be worried."

Both women laughed.

"Thanks for the call. I'll talk to you both later." Mary dropped her phone into her purse and walked through the yard toward Ethan. A scant bit of sunlight had broken through the clouds and was taking up residence on the porch, playing with the coffee-brown highlights in Ethan's dark hair. He looked serious and sexy, dressed in all black, the features in his face all angles and sharpness with a tigerlike stare. Her heart in her throat, Mary climbed the porch steps and sat beside him on the bench.

"Taking a walk?" he asked, his tone rigid.

"Just back from City Hall and a meeting with the caterer and waitstaff. They're really thrilled with the barbecue." She tried to ignore the way his gaze moved over her in a possessive, animal-like way. "The tasting you requested is today at one-thirty. If that works with your schedule."

He shook his head. "I don't need a tasting. I trust your instincts."

"Last night you said—"

"I wasn't talking about food last night, Mary."

His words stunned her, and his reckless, impenetrable gaze had heat coiling through her. Since he had wanted so much to avoid talking about their situation last night, she'd thought to grant him the same courtesy today, but he looked anything but calm, cool and forgetful, so she lifted her chin and said, "Do we need to discuss what happened last night?"

"Only if you want to continue where we left off," he said with a bluntness that matched hers.

Mary's nerves dropped away completely, and the no-

nonsense businesswoman with an attitude took over. She had been open to him in more ways than one last night, and he was the one who'd walked away. She didn't want to play games anymore, back and forth and want and don't want—it was b.s. "All I want right now is to do my job. The best damn job anyone's ever seen."

His eyes glittered with ire. "I have no doubt you'll succeed in that."

"And after I've finished this job, I want to leave here. I want to go back home and..." She paused, unable to finish her sentence. Why couldn't she finish that sentence?

"And?" he asked.

She would go back home and work as she always had, with no more interruptions or complications. No doubt, just like Ethan.

The frustration in her tone was obvious. "Would you like the tasting or should I cancel it?"

"I'll be there. One-thirty, right?"

She nodded and stood. "It's going to be at Fanfare restaurant in town, right on Main Street. Easy to find." She headed off toward the barn. Another shower sounded good, thirty minutes under hot water to clear her head and retune her attitude.

"I'll come by the barn to pick you up at one," Ethan called after her, making Mary stop in her tracks and whirl around to face him. "We can walk this time. No more horses."

"We?" she uttered hoarsely. "No, I don't need to be there. The staff will write down everything you like and don't like and report back to—"

"I want you there," he said, reclining on the bench, looking like the CEO of the world. "And at least until the end of the barbecue tomorrow, you work for me."

Without realizing it, the catering staff at Fanfare had romanticized an event that should have been nothing more than a business meeting. On the walk over, Mary had imagined that she and Ethan would stand at one of the prep stations in the restaurant's kitchen and sample a variety of dishes, writing down their thoughts on a piece of scratch paper in between bites, then they would thank the staff for their service and get out of there. Later, Mary would call the head chef and discuss what worked for the client and what didn't.

This was normally how it was done on the mainland, but clearly things were taken to an entirely different level on Mackinac Island when a hotshot millionaire was throwing a party for the island's upper crust.

On the restaurant's cozy deck overlooking the lake, a table had been dressed with exquisite white linens, funky blue plates, silver, wineglasses and frosted beer glasses.

"I feel like I should've worn a tie," Ethan said with a sardonic grin as he was seated at the table.

"Me, too," replied Mary.

"No. You look too good in that dress."

She smiled.

Taking in the elaborate scene before him, Ethan raised one dark brow at her. "Are you sure they're going to be able to pull off a beach barbecue?"

She tossed him a mock frown as the waitstaff poured

samples of wine and beer. "Are you questioning my abilities, Mr. Curtis?"

Lifting a mug, he gave her a silent toast. "I'd be a fool."

"Damn right." In spite of herself, she grinned at him as several dishes were set before them. "How about we taste and see?"

Amusement glittered in his eyes at the unintended double meaning in her words. "You make me crazy, you know that?"

"Right back at ya, Curtis."

Each item the staff laid before them was whimsical and over-the-moon delicious. Grilled whitefish and chips wrapped in paper, sweet-potato fries with a killer dipping sauce, salads, pork, chicken, desserts. And they sampled it all, along with fresh-squeezed lemonade, interesting wines and rich beer.

At long last, Ethan sat back in his chair and sighed. "I approve."

Mary laughed as she tried to get up from the table. "I thought you might."

After thanking the staff, they walked back to The Birches, thankful for the exercise as they were both stuffed to the gills. Several times, Ethan reached out to take Mary's hand, then stopped himself. They weren't a couple. Sure, there was an intense sexual attraction between them, unfinished business that he wanted to see to, taste again—damn, he couldn't get last night out of his head—but he was kidding himself if he thought they'd just been on a date, that they were starting a romantic relationship.

Once they were in the driveway, Ethan followed her to the barn and paused at the door. Mary's cheeks were flushed and she looked relaxed and satisfied with their day. She took off her sandals and stood there in her virginal white sundress, the same need he'd seen last night in her eyes—the same need that was no doubt echoed in his.

"I think I'm a little tipsy," she said, opening the door.

"There's nothing wrong with that."

She laughed. "It's three o'clock in the afternoon."

"Are you going to be operating any heavy farm machinery this afternoon?"

"No."

"Then you're fine."

"Thanks for walking me to my door, so to speak, but I'm good from here."

Cursing, he leaned against the door frame, feeling frustrated and dense. "Why the hell are we fighting this?"

She shrugged. "I don't think I am."

"Fine. Why am I fighting this?"

"Because you hate me?"

"No, I don't think that's true anymore." He reached out and took her hand. "In fact I don't think that was ever true. I think it's quite the opposite and that's why I'm fighting it." He took her other hand and pressed them behind her back, leaned in and kissed her gently, sensually on the mouth. "Come on," he uttered, leading her inside.

"No more games, Ethan," she said, her tone fragile for the first time since they'd met.

"No." He shook his head, led her up the stairs, but halfway there his need to kiss her, taste her, had him pulling her into his arms.

"The bed…" she uttered hoarsely.

Ethan nuzzled her neck, the curve of her ear, making her moan. "We'll get there."

Eleven

Somehow they stumbled up the stairs, clothes marking their way like Hansel and Gretel's breadcrumbs. Mary clung to Ethan like a rag doll, covering his mouth and neck with hungry kisses as he led them into the bedroom and onto the down comforter. She only knew her shirt and bra were off when her warm back met the cool, soft down and when Ethan lowered himself on top of her, the hair on his chest tickling her, and the delicious, hot weight of him making her heart jump with excitement.

Her skin felt as if it was on fire, itchy, needy, and she couldn't get him to touch her everywhere at once, so she had to force herself to relax as he lazily kissed her throat and breasts, nuzzling one nipple with his nose and cheek until Mary could hardly stand the torture and he finally gave in and suckled her deep into his mouth, tugging at the flesh with his teeth. She was in a dream—she had to be—but she didn't want to be. No matter how she and Ethan had begun, there was real, honest-to-goodness affection here. She was really falling hard for him, and she desperately wanted him to make love to her.

He found her mouth again, and as his hands took over, kneading the undersides of her breasts, cupping them, feeling their weight, slowly circling the firm peaks with his thumbs, Mary moaned, plunging her fingers into his thick hair.

His jeans and the small scrap of cotton at her hips were all that separated them, and Mary couldn't stand it. With deft fingers, she flicked the button and slid down his zipper, her hand delving inside to feel him, hold him, make him as insane with desire as she was.

Ethan sucked in a breath as her fingers wrapped the hard, solid length of him, and Mary smiled as he continued to kiss her. He was like silk, pulsating, hot, steel-hard silk, and she ached to have him inside her. As she stroked him, Ethan hooked his thumbs under the waistband of her underwear and slipped them down far enough that Mary could easily wriggle out of them. This was no sweet love scene; they wanted each other in a primitive way. They wanted to be connected, and Mary reveled in the fact that she felt like a horny teenager at the ripe old age of twenty-nine.

Ethan broke away for one second to pitch his pants to the floor, and when he returned, Mary pushed him back on the bed. She felt sexy and strong and wanted to climb on top of him and take what she wanted, be in control, and Ethan lay back and allowed her that, his hands instantly finding her hips.

She kneaded his chest with her hands, rolled his nipples between her fingers until his erection looked like a marble pillar, then she lifted up off him, pressed her hips forward and sank down until the curls between her legs met the coarse hair at his center.

Ethan uttered a curse, a deep throaty sound that went with the thrust he met her with. "Mary, I don't—"

"Want this?"

A deep, almost wounded chuckle escaped him. "Are you kidding? No, I don't have any protection."

"I do," she said breathlessly.

"You do?"

She pushed off him, her smooth legs brushing against his hair-roughened ones as she grabbed a foil packet from the bedside table drawer. "I'm not going to pretend I didn't want this to happen," she said, grinning down at him. "I came prepared."

Ethan reached for the packet, but Mary wanted to do it herself, wanted to feel the latex as it slid over him, wanted to place him inside her again. After feeling so out of control for so long, she needed this, and for once Ethan let her take what she needed, let her slide back down over him, let her place his hands on her breasts as she rode him, her hips swiveling and thrusting as she tried to feel him from every angle.

"Tell me," Ethan whispered, one hand trailing down her belly to the spot where they were joined, where wet heat made their movements quick and intensely pleasurable. "What do you want?"

Through gritted teeth, Mary cried out, "Yes, right there. Touch me there."

Ethan's fingers moved and played until Mary's head dropped back and her breasts rose and fell. She let him take over, one hand gripping her hips, rocking her back and forth, deeper and deeper, the other hand nestled between them, his middle finger flicking the tender button hidden inside until waves of pleasure so intense Mary could hardly breathe washed over her. Her hands slipped to his chest as he pumped furiously beneath her, guttural sounds erupting from his throat as he followed her over the edge.

Exhaustion flooded her and she collapsed on top of him, tears filling her eyes. She lay there, her heart thudding against his chest, and wondered what she'd been doing for the past two years besides working and remaining separate from the world. She'd never realized just how lonely she'd been, spending her time, energy and focus on the business. She'd completely cut herself off from living.

Ethan slid out from under her, and she gave him her back so they were spooning. It felt so good, so right to be held like this by him. How that was possible, after all they'd been through, she didn't know, but it was obvious to her that they might have a chance together.

Ethan trailed kisses down her back, down, down, raking his teeth against the sensitive spot right above her buttocks. Electric currents shot through Mary's weak limbs, and she uttered a playful, "What do you think you're doing?"

"I'm not done."

"Not done with what...oh."

He flipped her over and sat poised above her, staring down at her with eyes that glittered blue fire, his erection brushing against her leg, hard once again.

Laughing weakly, she grabbed the covers and hauled them up and over her head. "Can't. Tired."

"Mary," he began wickedly. "Do you actually think a few inches of cotton is going to stop me?"

With a little pleasurable scream, Mary saw Ethan appear at the bottom end of the covers, his gaze ravenous as he started at her ankles and crawled toward her, his mouth planting soft, wet kisses up her calves, knees and finally her inner thighs.

"You don't have to do a thing," he whispered, his mouth poised between her now widespread thighs.

Her fingers delving immediately into his hair, Mary lifted her hips tentatively. How could she resist? His head was down, the muscles in his shoulders flexing as he gripped her buttocks. His mouth was like heaven, his tongue...

"Ethan..."

He started slowly at first, just gentle laps at her sensitive sex, long, slow licks from hood to the opening of her body. But Mary's body responded quickly, writhing beneath him, twisting, her fingers leaving his hair to find herself. Ethan said something sexy and dirty as she opened the slick, hot folds at her core, then nuzzled and suckled at the taut bud that ached so badly. Following her rhythm, his pace quickened, moving with the thrust of her hips, until she arched her back and called out raw, insatiable moans over and over again, shuddering against his mouth.

Completely exhausted now, Mary curled over on her side and released a heavy, satisfied sigh, even smiling lazily when Ethan lay facing her on his side.

"I want to stay," he said.

"The bed's too small," she joked.

He draped one muscular thigh over her hips, pulling himself closer. "Is it?"

And they fell asleep that way.

The weather had been sketchy all morning, but miraculously by eleven o'clock the sun had pushed its way through the clouds and had started to warm the sand. Right alongside the staff, Mary helped set up tables, chairs, chaises and umbrellas, all in festive shades of blue-and-white stripes. The beach had been combed beautifully, leaving only the whitest, softest sand for their party, and when noon hit and the guests began to arrive, Mary breathed a sigh of relief. Despite the morning gloom and a night of amazing sex that had left her bone weary, she'd pulled it off.

Dressed in a simple though elegant navy-blue sundress and white hat, Mary walked from one station to another, making sure the drinks were flowing and the food was getting out in a timely manner. Barring one strange and obviously experimental plate of baked-bean custard that she immediately had the waiter send back to base camp, everything looked perfect.

Just as she was inspecting the barbecue grills and the delicious scents wafting from each, Ethan came up behind her and took her hand. She smiled instantly at his touch, and a warm sensation came over her heart as she recalled this morning, waking up together in a haze of touchy, feely, romantic sweetness, complete with breakfast and a killer make-out session at the door as they each complained about how late they were going to be but not really giving a damn.

"Twenty minutes into the party and I have two potential clients flying to Minneapolis next week for meetings," he said, brushing a kiss to her ear. "You're amazing."

He looked calm, relaxed and deadly handsome in white pants and black polo shirt, and Mary felt a strange sense of pride, as if they were actually together. "It's not me, it's the mojitos," she joked.

"No, it's you," he insisted, his blue eyes flashing with admiration. "Or maybe it's me around you."

"That's a nice thing to say," Mary said a little shyly, trying to ease her hand from his in case anyone was watching them. She didn't want to give anyone the wrong idea, especially Ethan. She had never been the kind of woman to have expectations, and no matter how much she wanted to curl into this man and whisper her feelings against his chest, she wasn't about to lay that kind of pressure on him. She may have come to a realization last night about what she had been missing, what she wanted now and how they'd both been stuck in a past that had ruled their actions. But Ethan might not have come to any realizations except that the two of them had just had great sex.

Whatever his beliefs, Ethan held firm to Mary's hand as they walked over to the bar, greeting guests along the way. It was odd. In all the years Mary had been one of NRR's partners, she'd never felt like an actual wife to a client, or wanted to be, until today. For brief moments she even caught herself imagining that she and Ethan were a couple as they circled the crowd.

"I should go and speak with the chef," she told Ethan after about twenty minutes of crowd watching. "We're running low on a few things."

Ethan nodded but didn't release her hand immediately. "Before you go, I have to ask you something."

"Okay."

"I feel like an ass—a romantic ass."

"A whole new thing for you?"

"You bet." Chuckling, he drove a hand through his hair. "Will you stay with me tonight?"

Pleasure circled her belly, and she grinned at him. "I seem to remember us agreeing to something…after the party ended."

He gave her a mock scowl. "No idea what you're talking about."

"Sure you do. Should I refresh your memory?"

"If you say one word about that conversation, I'll have to take drastic action."

Biting her lip to keep from laughing, she said, "After the party ended we were both supposed to—"

Before she could say another word, Ethan hauled her into his arms and kissed her hard and quick. "Don't make me take this to an obscene level in front of all these people," he warned against her mouth. "I'll ruin my reputation."

Mary laughed, a warm, rich sound that totally conveyed how happy he was making her in that moment. "Wasn't I supposed to take off just as soon as the last guest departed?"

"Oh, you asked for it," he said wickedly, taking her hand and slipping behind the bar where it was shady and devoid of party guests.

In seconds Mary had her arms around his neck as he kissed her with all the passion of the night before. When they finally came up for air, Ethan's eyes were glazed and hot and his voice was ragged with emotion. "Whatever we have going here, I want more of it."

All she could do was kiss him, passionately and without holding back.

He held her face in his hands. "Tell me you want that, too."

"I want that, but I'm a little scared."

"Of what?"

"All that's happened."

"That's over, Mary. Can't we decide to forget about it and leave it in the past?"

"I think we've both left too much in the past. Don't you think it's time to deal with it?"

His brow furrowed with frustration just as a loud trill erupted from Mary's pants pocket. With a quick look of apology, she grabbed her cell phone and flipped it open. "Hello."

"Mary, it's your grandmother."

"Grandmother, how are you?"

"Your grandfather has died."

Her heart sunk into her stomach. "What?"

"The funeral is Tuesday. You'll be here?"

"Yes, of course," she said quickly, uncomfortable with her grandmother's unemotional way of giving news. "How did it—"

"I will see you Tuesday," Grace continued brusquely. "St. Agnes, downtown. 10:00 a.m."

She hung up almost immediately after Mary said that she would see her at the church. Still in shock, Mary gripped the phone in her fist and stared at the sand.

"What's wrong?" Ethan asked gently.

"My grandfather died." Why was she feeling so blown away? She and Lars Harrington had never been close, but for some reason the news of his death reminded Mary of her mother's death, and of how short life really was.

"I'm sorry," Ethan said soberly. "How did it happen?"

"I have no idea."

He didn't push her for more. "When are you leaving?"

"Right away. Tonight."

He nodded. "I'm going with you."

"No," she said quickly, not sure why she didn't jump at the offer, but sensing in her gut that Ethan Curtis around her family right now might not be the greatest idea. "You have business to finish up here, people to see and deals to make. It's the reason why we came to Mackinac Island in the first place."

"All of that can wait a few days."

She eased away from him, from his embrace and the intimacy they'd shared only moments ago. "And lose momentum? No way. It was our plan, anyway, that I was going to leave today and you were going to stay. Let's stick with the plan, for now anyway."

Ethan wasn't a mysterious man; he said what he thought and didn't apologize for it. With an understanding but not altogether amused grin, he said, "You're almost as good at this as me."

"Good at what?"

"Pretending you don't give a damn."

They said nothing further as they walked back into the eye of the party.

The cemetery looked like an English garden, with buckets of daisies and vases of tulips and roses everywhere you looked. The woman next to Mary at the grave site had been nervous about what to say to Lars Harrington's granddaughter. She had bypassed the usual offers of sympathy and instead had gone on to explain that Sunday was the heaviest day for visitors to the cemetery, and that all the guilty relatives brought flowers. After a quick, tight-lipped smile to the woman, Mary had moved to the opposite side of the grave, to stand alongside her grandmother, aunt and cousins.

As the priest spoke, Mary gripped the stems of her lilacs—a flower her grandmother had always called "peasant flora" as they grew in just about anyone's backyard—recalling the day that she and her father had buried her mother. The weather had been far better than today, full sunshine and a heavy breeze, but the mood felt similar and, Mary noticed, some of the same crowd was there. But no one except Mary and Hugh had shed a tear that day, no one had left that cemetery broken the way they had.

Staring at the casket as it was lowered into the ground, Mary wondered if she'd actually healed from that whole ordeal: the illness and the loss. She'd always been so worried about fixing her father and helping him to get over his grief that she hadn't even looked at her own. No wonder she'd allowed herself to take that deal of Ethan's—she'd been a little out of her mind.

Ethan. Warmth spread through her and she wrapped her arms around herself. She missed him, missed sparring with him, lying in his arms, feeling alive. It had been a few days since she'd spoken to him, since he'd kissed her goodbye at the ferry and returned to the island.

Mary glanced up and spotted Tess and Olivia standing next to the woman who'd voiced the inappropriate cemetery comment. The two women looked quiet and sad, and even though she hadn't asked them to attend, Mary was thankful for their presence and support. And they weren't the only ones offering their support, Mary noticed as she shifted her gaze to the back of the crowd behind her partners.

Conservatively dressed in a black suit and bright-blue tie, Ethan Curtis stood apart from all the others, staring at her, his gaze solemn as Bible verses were read. At first, Mary felt a jump of excitement at the sight of him, then beside her, her grandmother opened her purse and noisily slipped out a tissue, which she used to dab her eyes. This probably wasn't good. Grace wouldn't want him here and might create a scene.

As soon as the service ended, Mary hustled over to him. He took her hand and kissed it. "I thought you might need…something. I wasn't sure exactly what, so I came instead."

"Thank you," she said, wanting to curl into his arms and let him comfort her. But she knew this wasn't the time or the place, and she needed to get him out of there before he was verbally attacked by her grandmother.

But unfortunately she wasn't quick enough.

"What is he doing here?"

It was as if a cold wind had blown in, encircling them like a tornado. Mary's grandmother walked up to them. She stared hard at Ethan, a sneer on her weary face.

"He came as a friend, Grandmother," Mary quickly tried to explain. "And—"

"He's no friend to this family," Grace snarled. "Your grandfather would be appalled."

"Grandmother, please—"

"You don't need to defend me, Mary," Ethan said calmly, then turned to Grace. "I was offering a little support to a friend, that's all."

Her eyes narrowed into nasty slits. "The blue-collar trash that took his company from him." She turned on Mary. "How could you allow this?"

"I didn't. I'm not. I—"

"Don't bother, Mary," Ethan said with a mild sigh before turning around and walking away.

"I'm surprised at you," Grace uttered to Mary when he was gone.

"And I wish I could say I'm surprised at you," Mary said tightly.

"You will not speak to me in that tone, young—"

"I understand that today is a difficult day, Grandmother," Mary said, feeling strong and in control with this woman for the first time in her life. "But I won't allow you to speak to my friends that way anymore. If you want a relationship with me, you'll need to restrain yourself in the future."

Leaving her grandmother standing there, mouth open, Mary went after Ethan. She caught up to him on top of the hill overlooking her grandfather's grave site. "I'm sorry. It's her grief talking."

"Then she's been grieving for a long time," he muttered.

"This is why I didn't want you to come here," she explained. "I knew she'd—"

"Stop trying to protect me, Mary. I don't need it."

"I'm not…" Even as she said the words, she knew they weren't true.

"Aren't you tired of it?"

"What do you mean?"

"Protecting everyone. Your father, your partners, your grandmother, me, yourself."

She stared at him unable to speak, her brain running a hundred miles an hour. Had he read her thoughts last night? How could he know that all of her life she'd been doing exactly this, hoping her interference would bring peace where there was chaos—and having no life of her own in the process. She could plan her work, her business years in advance, but could never see her personal future because she didn't think she deserved one.

"I have to go," Ethan said, mistaking her silence for indifference.

"No," she said sternly just as Olivia and Tess came toward them, waving.

"I'm so sorry, Mary," Olivia said sympathetically, placing an arm around her friend's shoulder. Then she noticed Ethan and gave him a curious smile. "Mr. Curtis. Hello. What are you doing here?"

"He took over my grandfather's company," Mary said quickly and without thinking. "But he was just leaving."

When Ethan's cold gaze found hers, she realized what she had said and how it had sounded. It was one thing to protect him, but to act ashamed of him... She wanted to explain, but with Tess and Olivia standing right there she knew it would have to wait.

Ethan nodded to both Tess and Olivia. "Ladies." Then turned and left.

Mary's heart sank.

"What happened here?" Tess asked.

Olivia grimaced. "Hope it wasn't something I said."

"No," Mary assured them, knowing it was about time to come clean with her partners. "I'm afraid it was something I said."

Twelve

"Yes, Mr. Valentine, I'll be there." Olivia rolled her eyes as she hung up the phone. "This is his third call in two days. The excessively rich can not only be bossy but paranoid, as well." She swiveled toward Mary and gave her a sheepish expression. "Sorry, Mary. I don't mean you."

It was quarter to five and they were all sitting in Olivia's office going over the appointments and events that were scheduled for the next two weeks. It was September and business was starting to really pick up.

As she sat beside Tess on the other side of Olivia's desk, Mary crossed and uncrossed her legs. "Hey, I'm not rich."

Tess looked up from her notes. "I thought your grandfather left you a small fortune."

"It still doesn't make me rich," Mary said on a laugh that sounded incredibly forced. "Comfortable, maybe—but I've found that rich is an attitude."

"I'll say," Olivia went on. "Just because this guy has a dozen or so women who'd do anything from shine his shoes to act as though they don't know where Darfur is just so he can feel like the smart one, doesn't mean he should expect the same from me." She snorted. "As if I would forget a meeting. The nerve."

"You'll make sure he gets a clue, Olivia, I have no doubt." Tess winked at Mary, who smiled in turn.

The three women had changed during the past several weeks—since the funeral and the three-hour dessert and coffee gab session they'd shared afterward. Exactly ten minutes after Ethan had walked away from her, Mary had broken down and confessed their relationship to Tess and Olivia.

The two hadn't been surprised, but they had asked, no pressure, if she'd wanted to talk about it. She did, and she had. Not that it had changed the situation any, but it had been moderately cathartic and had made Mary realize what she'd been missing in a friendship.

Both Tess and Olivia hadn't mentioned Ethan since, and she was beyond thankful for that because Ethan hadn't contacted her for two weeks except to send a check to NRR for services rendered. There hadn't been a note in the envelope, nothing that would make her think he missed her or had even thought about her at all. For her part, she'd called him to try and explain, but he'd refused to listen. Even so, she hadn't stopped thinking about him.

Tess closed her book with a sigh. "I think that's it. We're all going to be incredibly busy this month, so take every opportunity to relax."

"Agreed," said Olivia pulling out her Rolodex. "And I know just how to start the relaxation process."

Tess groaned. "I can't take another one of those seminars on How to Cool Your Cooperate Stress."

"Seriously," Mary agreed wholeheartedly. "I fell asleep at the last one and the group leader actually tousled my hair to get me to wake up. It was very freakish."

Shaking her head impatiently at both of them, Olivia explained, "I'm not talking about a seminar, I'm talking about Senõr Fred's—tonight." She wiggled her brows. "Spiciest salsa in town and dollar margaritas."

"Oh, I'm so in," Tess said without hesitation, standing up and heading out of the office. "Let me get my coat, finish up some paperwork and I'll meet you at reception in fifteen minutes."

"What about you, Mary?" Olivia asked. "I mean, can anyone really turn down a margarita?"

At that question, Mary wanted to laugh, but she didn't feel merry enough to make it happen. She could turn down a margarita, and pretty much anything alcoholic for the next nine months. She was back to where she'd started, with a pregnancy test hidden behind the rolls of toilet paper under the sink. And this time, she'd actually missed her period.

She scrubbed a hand over her face. How was she going to tell Ethan, or not tell him?

"I'd love to come," Mary said finally, feeling slightly

sick to her stomach at the thought of salsa and chips and happy hour chaos. "But I think I'll stick to soda."

Olivia smiled and shrugged. "Okay."

"But if you two end up completely hammered," Mary said, gathering up her notes and grinning. "Consider me your designated driver."

Dr. Eleanor Wisel was a kind, grandmother type of Ob/Gyn with cool hands and warm instruments and a penchant for delivering news with her eyes closed. Dramatic effect? Who knew, but it was exactly how she'd told Mary that yes, she was indeed pregnant.

With a prescription for prenatal vitamins stuffed in her purse and a small plastic bag of coupons, information and dates for future appointments hanging from her wrist, Mary walked out of the office building and across the parking lot toward her car. Her insides had stopped shaking long enough for her brain to start processing what all this could mean. She didn't have to worry about money or a future for this child—she had her business and the trust. She didn't have to worry about loving this baby, she already felt totally in love with him or her. But what she did have to worry about was the father. She had to tell him, of course, but things were so crazy right now, would it be better if she waited?

She opened her car door and was about to climb in when she heard her name being called across the parking lot. Her skin prickled and her heart raced, and she quickly tossed her free bag of goodies into her car and slammed the door. When she looked up again, he was there, looking incredibly handsome in jeans, a white button-down shirt and a gray brushed-wool blazer. She found herself fascinated with his features, wondering would her baby have his eyes or hers? His hair color or hers? His roguish smile or her quirky one?

"What are you doing here?" he asked in a tone he usually reserved for employees.

"Seeing a doctor."

Concern etched his features and he took a step closer to her. "Why? What's wrong?"

"Nothing." Why did he have to smell so good? All she wanted to do was fall forward, rest her forehead on his chest, tell him how much she missed him and that everything that happened the day of her grandfather's funeral was a stupid misunderstanding. "I'm perfectly healthy."

He looked relieved.

"And what are you doing here?" she asked, suddenly aware of the pregnancy packet laying on the back seat in full view.

"I had a meeting in the building next door, and I saw your car."

"Right," she said, patting the Mustang she'd have to get rid of now in favor of an SUV or something more child friendly.

"Well, it's been interesting." He looked ready to take off, but Mary was not about to let him leave without at least starting the groundwork for a decent future relationship.

"Ethan, I want to apologize for what happened at the funeral—"

He put up a hand to stop her. "No need."

"No, there is a need. What happened was a misunderstanding."

Beside them, a woman was getting into her car, tossing her purse and effects into the back of the car, just as Mary had done a few minutes earlier. But she was not just any woman, Mary realized, her stomach roiling sickly as she turned her head and tried to go unnoticed by the woman she had chatted with in the waiting room of Dr. Wisel's office.

"Oh, hey, there."

Too late.

Mary gave the woman a quick wave and a very tight-lipped smile as she silently begged her not to say anything more.

The woman waved, utter glee in her eyes at having heard good news today, as well. "See you later, and good luck with your baby."

Her heart in her shoes, Mary nodded as they woman got into her car and shut the door. "You, too."

She didn't want to look at him, afraid of what she'd see in his dark-blue gaze: horror, disgust, disappointment. It would be something she'd always remember, but she wasn't a coward, and she faced her child's father with a proud lift of her chin.

"Baby?" he repeated, his face registering utter shock.

"It looks that way. It's very early."

"But…how is that possible? I wore a—"

"I know."

"And the first time we had nothing at all and…well, nothing happened."

"I know."

He looked away, scrubbed a hand over his chin. "God, a baby. Your baby."

"Our baby," Mary couldn't stop herself from saying. She wasn't about to beg, but she loved the guy and she wanted him to want this child and her, too.

"Oh, Mary," he said with a softness she'd only heard when she was in his arms, when he kissed her. "Were you going to tell me?"

"Of course I was going to tell you," she assured him. "But you weren't taking my calls—"

"I would've taken this one."

"I had some things to think about first, some decisions to make—"

He went white as paper. "You're going to…to have it, right?"

Her heart leaped into her throat. How could he even think… "Yes."

He released a heavy sigh. "But you were going to wait to tell me?"

Around them people slammed doors and cars pulled in and out of their spaces. "Ethan, again, we haven't spoken in two weeks. I didn't know if we'd ever speak again the way you were ignoring my phone calls."

"I was pissed."

"I know."

"I had every right to be."

He did. "Okay."

"But that doesn't mean my feelings for you changed."

Mary felt her breath catch in her throat. What did that

mean? What feelings? Besides attraction and a strange friendship?

He continued, "That doesn't mean I didn't think about you every damn minute and want to be with you, around you, inside you."

"Ethan," she uttered, shaking her head.

"I have to know something, Mary."

"Okay."

"Are you ashamed of me, too?"

"What are you talking about?"

"What you did at the funeral—or what you didn't do. Your grandmother treated me like dirt and you stood there."

"You're right. I was an idiot. At first. But after you left, I told her off."

He didn't look as though he wanted that answer, he was still so angry—at her, and maybe at his life and past. "You couldn't get rid of me fast enough around Olivia and Tess."

Sighing, she leaned against the car. "That had nothing to do with shame, Ethan."

"What was it then?"

"I didn't want my partners to know about you."

He looked triumphant. "Exactly."

"No, not exactly. I didn't want them to know that I had allowed myself to be blackmailed by you, that I went to work for you afterward and then that I—" she swallowed "—fell in love with you in Michigan. If I'm ashamed of anyone, it's myself."

"For loving me?" he asked.

She studied him hard. "I'm coming clean here,

Ethan. I'm admitting my failings, how I've screwed up. I should have found a different way to help my father, or allowed him to find a way out himself. I know that all I've ever done is try to keep the peace, take care of everyone else but myself. Then I used it as an excuse to stay away from relationships with people." She looked heavenward. "But no more. I'm done with that. I have a child on the way, and I'm going to teach her by example to run headfirst into life and embrace it, and that the world's problems are not hers to solve." She looked at Ethan. "What are you going to teach her?"

Mary had hoped that her words, her own admission of past failures would jar him, make him see what a fool he'd been and how releasing the past was his only way to have a real future. But he wasn't ready for that, and she had to accept the fact that maybe he never would be.

"I have plenty to teach," he said proudly.

"The art of the deal?"

"There's nothing wrong with being ruthless in business matters—"

"Business matters?" She shook her head, disappointed. "You still don't understand what happened with us—or take any responsibility for it, do you?"

"If we're talking about the bargain—"

"Of course we are."

His chin set, his eyes blazing blue fire, he said, "I did what I had to do."

Mary laughed bitterly as she opened her car door and climbed in. "You know, with how brilliant you are, I'd have thought that by now you'd have come up with a far more creative answer. That one's getting a little tired, and frankly so am I," she said before closing the door in his face.

Ethan Curtis wasn't a big drinker, never packed up his troubles and headed to the nearest bar. Instead he preferred to solve his problems in a clear and rational way. Even in personal matters, this method worked well for him. Today, however, clear and rational just didn't exist.

He drove through the stone gates of the Days of Grace Trailer Park and past the office to the mobile home he couldn't seem to stay away from. The one-bedroom home seemed to stare back at him, wondering why he kept returning to a place that held such bad memories.

Ethan reclined his seat and shut his eyes, remembering the sound of his father cracking open another beer from his second six-pack, hearing the squeak of springs as the old man dropped down on the ratty couch before hurling beer caps at Ethan, along with a few choice words about how Ethan was the real reason his mother had left them.

Why the hell did he keep coming back here? Did he like torture? Did he feel he deserved it?

A loud knock on the window had Ethan awake and alert in seconds and he stared out the side window at the man who now owned the trailer. Still a little foggy with memory, Ethan pressed the button to his left, and the window dropped slowly.

The man had no baseball cap on this time and looked like a badass with his bald head, Iron Maiden T-shirt and sinister expression, but when he spoke there was no anger in his tone, only interest. "Is there a reason you like to park in front of my place or are you just a freak?"

"I used to live here."

The man's brows shot up. "Did you now?"

"With my mother and father—well, actually just my father."

"Yeah, I know about that." The man scratched his neck, said thoughtfully, "I got a boy myself. Teenager. Crazy at that age, but he's real smart. All As, every subject. Maybe he'll go to a good college and get a fancy car like yours."

"Maybe."

"That's why I moved here," the guy confessed. "For him, so he could go to the best public school in the city."

Ethan stared at the guy. He didn't have much, and he seemed to know the curse of a woman walking out on him or maybe never being around in the first place, and yet his biggest concern was his kid's future. Ethan hadn't had that kind of love and commitment from his own father, but he sure as hell wanted to be that kind of dad.

What the hell was he doing? Coming here, feeling sorry for himself when he had made a life that he should feel damn proud of. Mary had been right. He'd been lying to himself all along. The shame he felt for where he came from wasn't about the trailer—that was an easy excuse, and an easy place to throw the blame when he just didn't want to deal with the past. His shame came from a father who'd had no pride in himself and had blamed everyone else for his lot in life.

Kind of like Ethan.

He didn't need blue blood to feel worthy, and he didn't

need to be accepted by those people to feel real success. His real success was growing inside of Mary right now.

Ethan eyed the guy outside his window as he gave a quick wave to what was probably his teenage son on the porch. He'd never known the kind of love this man had for his kid, had no idea what it felt like, so to get it he'd forced a woman to create a child with him by threatening the one thing she loved.

"What a damn fool," he muttered.

"What was that?" the man asked, turning back.

"Just talking about myself, brother." Ethan took out his wallet. "Here." He handed the man a business card. "When your boy starts college, have him contact me."

The man read the card, then looked up impressed. "CEO?"

"Wouldn't have minded a leg up in the beginning," Ethan said. "We always have internships available."

"Appreciate it." The man pocketed the card, then gestured to the trailer. "You want to come in? We're just about to throw some steaks on the barbecue."

"Thanks." Ethan smiled. "But I think it's time I got out of here."

"Back where you belong?"

"That's right." He was only thinking about Mary and the baby when he said it.

Ethan drove away from the trailer park, knowing it was the last time he'd ever be back, realizing that if he wanted any future with the woman he loved and the child growing inside her, he had to leave the past where it was and look ahead to the future.

Thirteen

"I can't believe I'm going to be a grandpa."

Mary sat on the picnic blanket her father had laid out in the backyard beside the vegetable garden, a garden that was now going crazy with bushes of fragrant basil, vines of squash and pumpkin and rows of ripe cherry tomatoes.

"Well, it's true," she told him, taking a bite of her corned-beef sandwich.

He plunked down beside her, looking stronger than she'd seen him look in a year. His color was good, too, and when he spoke, his tone contained that rich, happy sound she remembered from her childhood. "Your mother would be so proud. I wish she could see…"

"I know. But she will, in her own way."

"I like that." He winked at her, then handed her a cookie. "I made these myself, chocolate chip."

She took a bite and sighed. "They're great. In fact, all of this food is wonderful. I may have to hire you to cater for the company."

He chuckled. "Sounds good. But let's wait until after I open my restaurant."

"You're opening a restaurant?"

"More like a roadside place. Sell my vegetables and offer some small meals, homemade ice cream, the cookies…" He grinned. "Who knows, it's still in the planning stages."

"Good for you."

He nodded, then shifting topics. "So, what are your plans? Are you going to stay in your apartment after the baby is born? It's pretty small."

"It is." She didn't know exactly what her plans were, only that she'd be okay and that this child would be loved beyond belief. "Oh, Grandmother called."

Hugh looked surprised. "Really? Even after the scene you told me about at the funeral?"

"She said she respects my choices—"

"She actually said that?"

Mary laughed. "I know. I was shocked, too. She even apologized and said my friends are my own business. Even after I told her who the father was. She wants me to move in with her, have the baby there."

"What did you tell her?"

"Thanks, but no thanks."

"Bet she wasn't too happy to hear that."

"No, but she said she understood and asked me to visit as much as I could."

Hugh munched on a carrot. "Boy, she's certainly changed her tune since her daughter married me."

"I guess so. She wants to be a part of my life and the baby's, and she said she was willing to let go of this feud with Ethan." Mary shrugged. "I'll believe it when I see it, but people have been known to change every once in a while, right? Even in small ways?"

"It's been known to happen," Hugh said, tossing aside his carrot and regarding her with serious eyes. "Did I say I'm not all that happy about the daddy myself?"

"You did." The sun was high in the sky, must be around one o'clock, she thought, reclining back on the blanket. "He made some mistakes, Pop. Some big ones, but then again so have I. So have you."

"Well, if sending that back to me was any indication of change, than perhaps you're right, lass."

Mary looked in the direction that her father was pointing. At the far end of the garden, where her mother had planted a circle of yellow roses, was the sculpture of mother and child that Hugh had risked so much in trying to get back.

"He gave that to you," she asked, stunned.

Hugh nodded. "Brought it by himself. We didn't say much to each other, but it was pretty decent of him."

Mary smiled to herself, knowing that for Ethan, coming to her father's house with that sculpture couldn't have been easy. He'd made a grand gesture.

When she looked up, her father was watching her. "You love him."

"Yes. I just hope that's enough. He's got some demons to exorcise, some new ideas to come to terms with and a life waiting for him. But I'm anxious to see what his next step will be."

Hugh lifted one grayish-blond brow. "And if he doesn't take a next step?"

"Then I'll be very sorry—" she lifted her chin, trying to ignore the ache in her heart "—but I'll survive."

It was Saturday morning around ten-thirty, and all three of the women of No Ring Required were working, sans receptionist. Business was crazy right now, and Mary, Olivia and Tess were all working overtime to accommodate their clients.

Tess stuck her head in Mary's office. She looked slightly anxious, unsure of how she wanted to say what she had come in there to say. "Mary, it's Mr. Curtis."

Her heart leaped into her throat. "Here?"

"No, he was on the phone."

"What line?" she asked, breathless.

"He's already hung up," Tess explained awkwardly. "But there's a message." She handed a slip of paper to Mary. "He asked if you'd meet him there."

"Asked?" Mary repeated.

Grinning, Tess nodded. "Good luck."

After Tess went back to her office, Mary stared at the address on the paper, her pulse pounding in her blood. After all they'd been through, she didn't want to go back to that place, especially now, but more than anything, she wanted to hear what Ethan had to say, so she stood up, grabbed her purse and headed out.

Ethan was actually nervous. Like a damn teenager asking out a girl he knew he was not even close to being good enough for. Thank God the baby shop wasn't packed with customers or he'd probably have to pay the owner to shut the place down for a while so he could really talk with Mary in private.

The bell over the door jingled, and he turned to see Mary walk in, looking so beautiful Ethan almost couldn't speak. Her blond hair fell in waves around her shoulders and she wore a cream linen pantsuit with sexy sandals and pale-pink toes.

He picked up a baby blanket from the railing of a nearby crib. "I think we should stay away from anything blue. Even if it is a boy."

With wary eyes she regarded him. "What am I doing here?"

"Sit." Grinning at the command that came so easily to him, he amended quickly, "Please."

She sat in the rocker next to him and waited.

"How are you?" he asked.

"Fine. Curious."

He nodded, knowing he needed to get to the point if he wanted to keep her attention. "Look, Mary, I get it now."

Her brows lifted. "Get what?"

"My hang-ups. All seven hundred of them. I get it. I forced you into a situation that was impossible, all for the sake of feeling like I was worth something. You have every right to be angry with me. But you have no right to be ashamed of yourself."

"I'm not."

"I'm glad."

She gave him a tight-lipped smile. "But thank you for saying that."

"Oh, honey," he said, dropping to his knees in front of her. "That's just the tip of the iceberg as far as confessions go."

Mary felt her pulse pick up speed as hope surged through her for the first time in weeks. Ethan's heart was open to her, completely. She could see it in his eyes, hear it in his voice.

He took her hand in his and kissed the palm. "I know after all I've done that asking you to love me again is asking a helluva a lot, but I'm asking anyway."

Her stomach flipped. She couldn't believe what he was saying. "You don't have to do this. If it's about the baby, you can be a part—"

"Mary, I love you. Finding out about the baby didn't change that fact, but it did force me to face what I've done, what I thought I needed and a past I just couldn't let go of."

Completely overwhelmed, Mary shook her head at him.

"What is it, sweetheart?" he asked, kissing her hand again so tenderly, so reverently it brought tears to her eyes.

"I just never thought we'd get here."

"But we did."

"I know and I'm so thankful."

"You wanted to know what gift I can give this child?" he said, reaching out to touch her belly.

Mary nodded, too emotional to speak.

"I can give the same gift our child's mother gave to me—love."

In that moment all Mary wanted to do was wrap her arms around Ethan and never let go. "I do love you, Ethan. So much."

He kissed her neck, her cheek, her eyelids. "I love you, too. Marry me?"

She laughed, insanely happy and so sure of her future. "Yes. Yes. Yes."

Ethan kissed her, a hungry, possessive kiss that she never wanted to end.

"Hi, there," came a feminine voice from behind them.

Still clinging to each other, Ethan and Mary glanced up and smiled sheepishly at the saleswoman.

"Are we shopping for ourselves or for someone else?" she asked.

Ethan reached in his pocket and took out the most beautiful yellow-diamond ring. He grinned at Mary as he slipped it on her finger. "What do you think, my soon-to-be Mrs. Curtis? Shall we do a little shopping?"

Mary kissed him squarely on the mouth and said happily, "I think it's about time."

* * * * *

Melita had been expecting a chaste quick kiss of the generic variety. But this kiss with Sully was the kind that sparked a dying flame to life. The kind of kiss you can't plan for. The kind of kiss memories are built on.

The memory of her murdered lover, Nemo, came to her then and she made a starved little noise in the back of her throat. She raised her arms and threaded her fingers through Sully's hair, pulled him closer. Felt his body settle, then melt into her.

In that instant her hunger for him grew, and his for her. She pressed herself to him with more urgency, and he responded in kind.

Melita came out of her kiss-induced memory of

Nemo with a start. "Wait a minute." She pushed Sully away from her. "You bastard!"

She spit two nasty words at him in Greek, then wiped his kiss from her lips.

"I thought you deserved some solid proof that I'm still in one piece." He started for the door. "The clock's ticking, honey. Come on, let's get out of here."

"That's it? You sucker me into kissing you, and that's all you have to say?"

"I'm sorry. How's that?"

He didn't sound sorry in the least. "You're—"

"Getting out of this godforsaken prison cell. Stop whining and let's go."

"Not if I was being shot at sunrise. Go. You deserve whatever you get if you walk out that door."

He turned back. "Freedom is what I'm going to get."

"A second of freedom before the guards in the hall shoot you." She jammed her hands on her hips. "And to think I was worried about you."

"If you're staying behind, it's no skin off my ass."

"Wait! What about our deal?"

"You just said you're not coming. Make up your mind."

"Have you forgotten we need a boat?"

"How could I? You keep harping on it."

"I'm not going without a boat. And those guards out there aren't going to just let you walk out of here. You need me and we need a plan."

"I already have a plan. I'm getting out of here. That's the plan."

"I should have realized that you never intended to

take me with you from the very beginning. You're a liar and a coward."

Of everything she had read, there was nothing in Sully Paxton's file that hinted he was a coward, but it was the one word that seemed to register in that one-track mind of his. The look he nailed her with a second later was pure venom.

He came at her so quickly she didn't have time to get out of his way. "You know I'm not a coward."

"Prove it. Give me until dawn. I need one more night to put everything in place before we leave the island."

"You're asking me to stay in this cell one more night...and trust you?"

"Yes."

He snorted. "Yesterday you knew they were planning to harm me, but instead of doing something about it you went to bed and never gave me a second thought. Suppose tonight you do the same. By tomorrow I might damn well be in my grave."

"Okay, I screwed up. I won't do it again." Melita sucked in a ragged breath. "I can't leave this minute. Dawn, Sully. Wait until dawn." When he looked as if he was about to say no, she pleaded, "Please wait for me."

"You're asking a lot. The door's open now. I would be a fool to hang around here and trust that you'll be back."

"What you can trust is that I want off this island as badly as you do, and you're my only hope."

"I must be crazy."

"Is that a yes?"

"Dammit!" He turned his back on her. Swore twice more.

"You won't be sorry."

He turned around. "I already am. How about we seal this new deal?"

He was staring at her lips. Suddenly Melita knew what he expected. "We already sealed it."

"One more. You enjoyed it. Admit it."

"I enjoyed it because I was kissing someone else."

He laughed. "That's a good one."

"It's true. It might have been your lips, but it wasn't you I was kissing."

"If that's your excuse for wanting to kiss me, then—"

"I was kissing Nemo."

"What's a nemo?"

Melita gave Sully a look that clearly told him that he was trespassing on sacred ground. She was about to enforce it with a warning when a voice in the hall jerked them both to attention.

She bolted away from the wall. "Get back in bed. Hurry. I'll be here before dawn."

She didn't reach the door before he snagged her arm, pulled her up against him and planted a kiss on her lips that took her completely by surprise.

When he released her, he said, "If you're confused about who just kissed you, the name's Sully. I'll be here waiting at dawn. Don't be late."

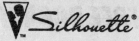

Romantic
SUSPENSE

**Sparked by Danger,
Fueled by Passion.**

Onyxx agent Sully Paxton's only chance of
survival lies in the hands of his enemy's daughter
Melita Krizova. He doesn't know he's a pawn in the
beautiful island girl's own plan for escape. Can
they survive their ruses and their fiery attraction?

*Look for the next installment in the
Spy Games miniseries,*

Sleeping with Danger
by Wendy Rosnau

Available November 2007 wherever you buy books.

REQUEST YOUR FREE BOOKS!

2 FREE NOVELS PLUS 2 FREE GIFTS!

Silhouette® Desire®

Passionate, Powerful, Provocative!

YES! Please send me 2 FREE Silhouette Desire® novels and my 2 FREE gifts. After receiving them, if I don't wish to receive any more books, I can return the shipping statement marked "cancel." If I don't cancel, I will receive 6 brand-new novels every month and be billed just $3.80 per book in the U.S., or $4.47 per book in Canada, plus 25¢ shipping and handling per book and applicable taxes, if any*. That's a savings of almost 15% off the cover price! I understand that accepting the 2 free books and gifts places me under no obligation to buy anything. I can always return a shipment and cancel at any time. Even if I never buy another book from Silhouette, the two free books and gifts are mine to keep forever.

225 SDN EEXJ 326 SDN EEXU

Name	(PLEASE PRINT)	
Address		Apt.
City	State/Prov.	Zip/Postal Code

Signature (if under 18, a parent or guardian must sign)

Mail to the Silhouette Reader Service™:
IN U.S.A.: P.O. Box 1867, Buffalo, NY 14240-1867
IN CANADA: P.O. Box 609, Fort Erie, Ontario L2A 5X3

Not valid to current Silhouette Desire subscribers.

Want to try two free books from another line?
Call 1-800-873-8635 or visit www.morefreebooks.com.

* Terms and prices subject to change without notice. NY residents add applicable sales tax. Canadian residents will be charged applicable provincial taxes and GST. This offer is limited to one order per household. All orders subject to approval. Credit or debit balances in a customer's account(s) may be offset by any other outstanding balance owed by or to the customer. Please allow 4 to 6 weeks for delivery.

Your Privacy: Silhouette is committed to protecting your privacy. Our Privacy Policy is available online at www.eHarlequin.com or upon request from the Reader Service. From time to time we make our lists of customers available to reputable firms who may have a product or service of interest to you. If you would prefer we not share your name and address, please check here. ☐

SDES07

HARLEQUIN®

Mediterranean NIGHTS™

*Not everything is above board
on Alexandra's Dream!*

*Enjoy plenty of secrets, drama and sensuality
in the latest from Mediterranean Nights.*

Coming in November 2007...

BELOW DECK

by

Dorien Kelly

Determined to protect her young son,
widow Mei Lin Wang keeps him hidden
aboard *Alexandra's Dream* under cover of
her job. But life gets extremely complicated
when the ship's security officer, Gideon Dayan,
is piqued by the mystery surrounding this
beautiful, haunted woman....

At forty, Maureen Hart suddenly finds herself juggling
men. Man #1: her six-year-old grandson, left with her
while his mother goes off to compete for a million dollars
on reality TV. Maureen is delighted, but to Man #2—
her fiancé—the little boy represents an intrusion on
their time. Then Man #3, the boy's paternal grandfather,
offers to take the child off her hands…
and maybe even sweep Maureen off her feet….

Look for

I'M YOUR MAN

by

SUSAN CROSBY

Available November wherever you buy books.

For a sneak peek, visit
TheNextNovel.com

HN88145

HARLEQUIN® Romance®

New York Times bestselling author

DIANA PALMER

Handsome, eligible ranch owner Stuart York knew
Ivy Conley was too young for him, so he closed his heart
to her and sent her away—despite the fireworks between
them. Now, years later, Ivy is determined not to be
treated like a little girl anymore…but for some reason,
Stuart is always fighting her battles for her. And safe in
Stuart's arms makes Ivy feel like a woman…his woman.

Winter Roses

Available November.

COMING NEXT MONTH

#1831 SECRETS OF THE TYCOON'S BRIDE—
Emilie Rose
The Garrisons
This playboy needs a wife and deems his accountant the perfect
bride-to-be…until her scandalous past is revealed.

#1832 SOLD INTO MARRIAGE—Ann Major
Can a wealthy Texan stick to his end of the bargain when he beds
the very woman he's vowed to blackmail?

#1833 CHRISTMAS IN HIS ROYAL BED—Heidi Betts
A scorned debutante discovers that the prince who hired her is the
same man who wants to make her his royal mistress.

#1834 PLAYBOY'S RUTHLESS PAYBACK—
Laura Wright
No Ring Required
His plan for revenge meant seducing his rival's innocent daughter.
But *is* she as innocent as he thinks?

#1835 THE DESERT BRIDE OF AL ZAYED—
Tessa Radley
Billionaire Heirs
She decided her secret marriage to the sheik must end…just as he
declared the time has come to produce his heir.

#1836 THE BILLIONAIRE WHO BOUGHT CHRISTMAS—
Barbara Dunlop
To save his family's fortune, the billionaire tricked his
grandfather's gold-digging fiancée into marriage. Now he
discovers he's wed the wrong woman!

SDCNM1007